The Figure in the Dusk

D1564960

*Also available in Perennial Library
by John Creasey:*

The Beauty Queen Killer
The Blind Spot
The Case Against Paul Raeburn
The Creepers
Death of a Postman
The Gelignite Gang
Give a Man a Gun

The Figure in the Dusk

John Creasey

PERENNIAL LIBRARY

Harper & Row, Publishers, New York
Cambridge, Philadelphia, San Francisco, Washington
London, Mexico City, São Paulo, Singapore, Sydney

A hardcover edition of this book was originally published in England under the title *A Case for Inspector West*. A hardcover edition of *The Figure in the Dusk* was published in the United States in 1952 by Harper & Brothers.

THE FIGURE IN THE DUSK. Copyright © 1952 by John Creasey. Copyright © renewed 1980 by Diana Creasey, Colin John Creasey, Martin John Creasey and Richard John Creasey. All rights reserved. Printed in the United States of America. No part of this book may be used or reproduced in any manner whatsoever without written permission except in the case of brief quotations embodied in critical articles and reviews. For information address Harper & Row, Publishers, Inc., 10 East 53rd Street, New York, N.Y. 10022. Published simultaneously in Canada by Fitzhenry & Whiteside Limited, Toronto.

First PERENNIAL LIBRARY edition published 1987.

Library of Congress Cataloging-in-Publication Data
Creasey, John.
  The figure in the dusk.
  Originally published under title: A case for Inspector West.
  I. Title.
PR6005.R517C37   1987   823'.912   87-45036
ISBN 0-06-080891-8

87 88 89 90 91   OPM   10 9 8 7 6 5 4 3 2 1

1

Murder on the Road

It was dusk, and the man moved from the side of the road, making Arlen start. His foot came off the accelerator and went onto the brake. The man stepped straight in front of him, dark, lean, long-haired. He didn't raise his hands or make any signal—just stopped and looked. Arlen's foot jammed down hard, and he pulled on the handbrake, but didn't think he could stop in time. The car stopped, jolting Arlen forward, and the man was still there, upright, unhurt.

"You damned fool!" Arlen's voice was squeaky, this had scared him so much.

The man smiled, raised his right hand in token acknowledgment, and strolled round to the door. He opened it without a word, and climbed in next to Arlen.

"You're going my way," he said.

"You—you must be crazy!"

"I can jump fast," the man said. "Which way are you going?"

Arlen made no answer, but wiped his forehead, and wished he didn't feel so cold. It was partly because of his alarm, partly because of the man's sneering, aggressive manner.

"There's no one in the way now," said the man. "You can drive on."

Slowly and deliberately, Arlen switched off the engine.

"That's right," he said. "I can drive on, when I'm alone. You get out."

"You misunderstand me; I'm coming for a ride."

Because it was dusk, the man's features were shadowy.

"Not with me," said Arlen.

He didn't know whether he could keep up the defiance, but having started, he couldn't very well give way. He took out his cigarette case, and as he opened it, a thin hand stretched out and plucked a cigarette.

"Thanks."

Arlen knocked the cigarette out of long fingers.

"Now, take it easy," said the man. "You'll make me angry if you go on that way, and I don't want to hurt you. Give me a cigarette."

"I'll be damned if—"

The stranger put his hand to his pocket, with such deliberation that Arlen broke off.

A gun appeared.

"Mind if I have that cigarette?"

Arlen's hands were unsteady, but he was still stubborn; he had always been an obstinate man. He closed the case and slid it back into his pocket, and was proud of the steadiness of his voice.

"If you think you can frighten me, you're all wrong. Get out and stay out."

"Listen," said the stranger. "And look."

It was a quiet country road, twenty miles from London. There were fields on either side, and

2

against the darkening sky the branches of oaks and beech, just coming into leaf, looked dark and somber. It was very quiet—until the shot rang out. The bullet passed a few inches in front of Arlen's eyes, and he imagined he could feel the heat of the shot. He flinched at the report and the flash, and felt an agonizing spasm of fear.

"Now I'll have that cigarette."

Arlen gave him one.

"Light."

Arlen thumbed his lighter.

"Thanks." The stranger leaned forward, and his eyes shone in the little light. "Where are you going?"

"I'm—I'm going home. I—"

"I guessed that, but where is home?"

"Chelsea, I—"

"I don't know what's come over you," said the passenger, "but you forgot to light your own cigarette. We're going the same way. You can drop me at Wimbledon Common—the Putney side. Then you can go home to your wife and family all alone and in one piece."

Arlen burst out: "You've got a nerve!"

"And you've some sense." The gun was in the pocket farthest away from Arlen, and the man himself edged against the door, as if he suspected that Arlen might try to strike him. "Let's get going."

Arlen started the engine and let in the clutch. As the car moved off, he frowned—partly because he realized that he had seen this man's face before. It wasn't familiar, but he'd seen it somewhere. The pendulous lower lip and the short upper lip made him feel certain. He stared straight ahead, thinking of that face and the way the man had looked, cold and unfeeling, when he had fired the shot.

This road was little used and went on for several miles before it ran into the outskirts of Kingston; after that it was a swift run along the dual carriageway by-pass, to Roehampton and Wimbledon Common. The by-pass would be busy.

As he drove steadily along this winding road, Arlen decided what he would do. Certainly he couldn't let an armed man stay free—the quicker the police dealt with him the better. He would go halfway along the by-pass as if he were going to obey, then jam on his brakes. As he would be prepared and the other taken unawares, there shouldn't be much trouble. He'd knock the man out, and then stop a passing motorist, and the police would soon be on the scene.

He didn't feel elated, he was far too nervous. The other was looking at him as if he could read his thoughts.

Arlen switched on the headlamps, for safety and for comfort; it wasn't good to be in the half light with this creature; that word sprang to mind, not man.

The lights shone on the windows of a cottage, a pale yellow sheen which disappeared, and the cottage showed for a moment against the skyline. A light was on, in one room.

Where had he seen this man before? Had he actually seen him in the flesh, or a picture?

"You've a nice car," the stranger said suddenly.

"It's all right."

"It's a fine car. These Austin Sheerlines take some beating. What's the price today?"

"About—about fourteen hundred," Arlen said.

"I wish I could afford to run round in a fourteen-hundred-pound car. You must be worth a pile of money."

"I—I get along."

Arlen shot a glance at the stranger, becoming more afraid. If the other thought he had a lot of money in his pocket, anything might happen. Arlen had twenty-nine pounds and some loose silver. His mind played tricks, and he thought of the other things he had of value. The gold cigarette case, gold lighter, gold watch—all Muriel's presents to him. "I know I shouldn't, darling, but I like you to have nice things."

"Mustn't you?" insisted the stranger, softly.

"Eh?"

"You're not very polite. I remarked that you must be worth a pile of money."

"No, not at all, I—I have heavy expenses to meet. I have, really." Now Arlen's tongue ran away with him. He had always known that he wasn't a brave man, now he had proof. "Home, my wife, three children; two of them are away at school; it costs a fortune these days, and what with income tax—"

The man opened his mouth and laughed, softly.

"You have a hard time, don't you? A beautiful wife—I bet she's beautiful—a big house, a fat income. I don't know why some men have all the luck and others don't get any. I've never had any luck."

Arlen didn't answer.

"We're getting near Kingston," said the stranger. "Don't do anything silly, will you?"

Arlen exploded: "All I want is to get rid of you!"

"You will, if you're careful," said the stranger. "Tell me about your wife. Is she beautiful?"

"She—"

"Got a photograph?"

5

"No, I—"

"Come on, I'll bet you have one close to your heart," said the stranger, and gave the soft laugh again.

He stretched out his hand and felt inside Arlen's pocket, pulling out his wallet as if by sleight of hand. He let it fall open. There was just sufficient light for him to see the money. That was why he had taken the wallet, of course.

Arlen felt panic tearing at him.

Long, bony fingers fiddled inside the wallet and drew out two photographs. It was too dark to see them, but the man put them close to his face, in pretense. Arlen felt a spasm of dread; the man was toying with him, cat and mouse; there was evil in him; this was a form of sadism. He gritted his teeth and his foot went harder on the accelerator.

"Steady," said the stranger. "You don't want to break our necks, do you? Turn left at the next corner."

"*Left?* It's straight on, to—"

"You heard me."

Arlen thought: "I won't do it." He pressed down his foot harder than ever. The stranger could do nothing while he was traveling at speed, dared not shoot while he was in control of the car. Go faster, faster! He swung round corners and passed a cyclist coming toward him; he saw the girl bump onto the grass verge, and thought she fell off her machine. Faster, faster! He caught a glimpse of a signpost at the extreme range of his headlamps, and it pointed left.

Then, swift as a picture flickering across the screen, he remembered why he thought he had seen this man before.

He reared back, in horror—and the stranger

clipped him on the side of the jaw. He felt the man take the wheel, leaning over him, felt the fenders scrape the hedge, then felt the car swing round to the left. It wobbled wildly, but the stranger steadied it. Hedge, narrow road, a heap of gravel and two tar barrels showed up in the glare—and then the man switched off the engine and they slowed down, astoundingly in the middle of the road.

Arlen grabbed at the door handle.

The man hit him again, savagely, and he gasped and relaxed his grip.

"You recognized me, didn't you?" said the stranger in a gentle voice. "That's just too bad."

Suddenly, he switched off the headlights, and it was now practically dark; to Arlen, it seemed pitch dark. He shifted his position and struck out wildly, hit the man somewhere, but did no harm. He struck again but only hit the far window; that hurt.

He saw a flash, heard a roar.

The tall, dark man with brown eyes took the money out of Arlen's pockets, then the watch, lighter and cigarette case, pulled a signet ring off his finger and, still not satisfied, searched in the other pockets until he found a case of keys.

Next, he opened his door, leaving Arlen slumping backward, blood from his head dripping to the back of the car. He rounded the car, opened the other door and dragged the dead man out. A few yards farther on was a gate leading into a field. He dragged the body to the gate and through; there was now no risk of its being seen by night.

He went back to the car, took the wheel, started the engine and, quite suddenly, gave the soft laugh which had frightened Arlen. He drove a little way, reversed, and soon reached the Kingston by-pass.

He swung onto it, and joined the stream of traffic racing toward London. The car behaved beautifully, and he was a good driver.

He reached Putney Hill. . . .

He reached Chelsea Town Hall and turned right, toward the river, until he found himself in one of the wide streets with graceful houses, near the river. He pulled up, switched on the roof light and glanced at a letter he had taken from Arlen's pocket. It was addressed: *W. Arlen, Esq.*, 7 Merrick Street, Chelsea, S.W.3, but the driver already knew that.

A couple walked along the street toward him. He opened his window, but did not look out. When they'd passed, he drove on, turned into Merrick Street; this was a high-class residential neighborhood. He went slowly along, until he passed a house with a hall light on, and the number 7 on the glass fanlight. He touched his forehead.

"I'll be seeing you soon," he said.

2

Burglary

"Of course there's no need to worry, Dennis," said Muriel Arlen. "Daddy's often as late as this. You go to sleep."

She stood by the open door of her son's room, smiling at a pair of rounded and anxious eyes, gray like his father's. At ten, Dennis was remarkably like his father. He had promise of the same curly fair hair, the same broad forehead and—although few knew this—the same stubborn temperament and earnest manner.

"He isn't often later than eight o'clock," said Dennis.

"He has been several times."

"But it's nearly half past nine now; I haven't been able to get to sleep, through worrying."

"Nonsense! Off you go!"

Muriel Arlen waved and laughed, and went out of the room, closing the door firmly.

Her expression changed as she walked away from the room toward the spacious landing. It was a Georgian house, roomy, comfortable and, under her guiding hand, charming and attractive; the house of wealthy people.

She hurried downstairs. The hall light was on. She stood looking at the front door, made a sudden decision and opened the door and looked up and down, but saw no sign and heard nothing of a car. She closed the door and went into a small room on the left of the hall; this was the morning room, where she spent most of her time. It was restful and pleasing. A bright fire warmed the April night, firelight flickered on the pale green of the walls and was caught by the glass in the frames of the water-colors, lending richness to the glasses and bottles which stood on a round table, ready for her husband's return. He was a creature of habit, and few things pleased him more than the drink they always had as soon as he was home.

The *Times* and *Telegraph* were folded on the arm of his chair. He liked his creature comforts, and Muriel indulged them. He was satisfied with the trappings of contentment; she believed he was actually contented.

On the top of the bookshelves in a corner recess were photographs of the family. She didn't look at them, but stood by the telephone, which was near his chair. Abruptly, she snatched up the receiver and dialed.

She stared into the fire, which glistened on her eyes; her lips were parted as if in excitement. After a long pause, a man answered.

"Hallo."

"Ralph," said Mrs. Arlen, "I'm so glad you're back."

"My sweet!" The man's voice was deep, and pleasant and low pitched. "Just a moment; I've dropped my cigarette." There was another pause, and through it faint sounds, which might have been voices. "Here we are, then! I'm dreadfully sorry I couldn't come this afternoon. I— Here! Don't say he's not coming home tonight, and we—"

"Ralph, he's not home, and I'm worried. There's been no message."

"I don't see why that should worry you," said the man. "If we'd known, I'd have come round again for a couple of hours. That husband of yours is just about the most inconsiderate devil I know. When are you going to—"

"Ralph, please. It's so unlike him."

"He's probably had a breakdown, and hasn't had a chance to telephone," said the man. "Don't worry, my darling."

She didn't answer.

"Muriel, there's no need to worry," the man said more emphatically. "No need on two counts—first because he'll turn up like a bad penny—nothing ever happens to men who're in the way—and second, because I don't like you worrying about him. The trouble with Wilfred is that he's a bad habit that's grown on you. You can't shake him off."

"I see," said Muriel despondently.

"Darling! I don't mean to upset you, but there isn't any need to worry. You know I always get savage when I think about him. You and I could—"

"Don't let's talk about that now. I can't help being worried. Dennis can't get to sleep because of it, and I—well, I always fly to you when I'm in trouble."

"Then keep on doing it," said Ralph. "Like me to come round?"

"You'd better not," she said. "He might be back at any time."

11

"That proves you know that you really needn't worry."

"I wondered if—"

"Wondered what?"

"I wondered if I ought to call the police."

"My darling, why on earth raise a scare because he's a couple of hours late? Hasn't he ever been late before?"

"Never, without sending me a message."

"There's one thing," said Ralph, in a bitter voice, "you can always depend on him, and set your watch by his coming and going. How I detest that man! I—sorry, my sweet. Feelings got the better of me. Look here, I'll call you in half an hour. If he hasn't turned up, we'll think about it again."

"No, I'll ring you," said Muriel.

He laughed.

"Because you know he'll probably be back by then, and wonder who's calling! You're not really worried, darling; you just wanted to talk to me."

"I *always* want to talk to you," said Muriel.

"Good-by, my darling."

"Give yourself a good strong gin," said Ralph. " 'By, precious."

She put down the receiver, but didn't move from the table. Fancied faces appeared in the fire: Wilfred's and Ralph's. She glanced up to the photographs, seeking Dennis's. The girls were older: twins of seventeen. They were old enough to understand, and from little things they had said she knew that they were sometimes puzzled by their father, and easily became impatient with him. Dennis was different; and Dennis's heart wasn't sound. But for Dennis, she would have left Wilfred years ago. The irony of it was that she'd conceived Dennis, hoping desperately that it would give

Wilfred what he most wanted and turn him into a human being instead of a kind of automaton.

She was as much a creature of habit as he; she normally wouldn't drink until he was home, but she now went across and poured herself out a drink; it didn't help. It was getting on for ten.

Ralph was quite right, the police would probably laugh at her. "Really, madam? *Two* hours late? An hour and three-quarters? Well, it isn't really serious, is it? If you will keep us informed."

She lit a cigarette.

In the mornings she was never really happy until Wilfred had left and she had a day of freedom ahead. She began to withdraw within herself when he was due home, and from the moment his car sounded outside she became frozen—a shell, talking, smiling, pretending, doing everything mechanically—and satisfying him, because that was all he needed to make him satisfied. Yet she could worry like this because some trifling accident or hold-up had delayed him.

"Ralph, it's nearly eleven, and he's not back yet."

"Good Lord! As you didn't ring before, I thought he'd shown up."

"Something must have happened."

"Not necessarily serious. You know, sweet, you've always regarded Wilfred as a paragon, but he might have a little blonde tucked away somewhere, and—"

"If he had, he'd leave her in time to be home, or send a message," Muriel said. "Don't be flippant about it."

"Sorry, darling. Shall I come round?"

"It wouldn't be wise, but I wish you could."

"Come and see me, then."

"You know I can't, tonight. It's Wednesday; the servants are still out. Ralph, ought I to telephone the police?"

"Well—I shouldn't think so yet, but if it will ease your mind, have a word with them. I wish—"

"Yes?"

"Never mind," said Ralph gruffly.

"But I do mind."

"Then I wish you were jumping for joy because he was late, and you were having an evening on your own."

"It's—Dennis."

"Isn't he asleep yet?"

"Yes, but—"

"You know, darling, the trouble is that it's too much of a strain. I've noticed it lately. You're jumpy and edgy most of the time; living with him is getting on your nerves. That, and *not* living with me. Don't go on too long, sweet. I know you think he'd never divorce you, but you can't be sure with the righteous. He'll probably call you a scarlet woman, and—oh, I'm sorry. But you know how I feel."

"Yes, darling," said Muriel. "I think I'll wait until midnight, and if he isn't back then, call the police."

"Do that," said Ralph.

She went upstairs to Dennis's room. He was sleeping on his back, had a lovely color, and looked fit and strong. His curly hair was rumpled; both the girls had straight hair. Dennis had the good looks, too, although none of the children was really plain. She stood looking at him for several minutes, then went downstairs. She had never known such a long evening. She poured herself out another gin and orange, and tried to read, but couldn't settle. Time passed so slowly. She was torn between the two attractions: home and Dennis, and Ralph. It was easy to understand why Ralph was so impatient; an intolerable situation had been getting worse for three years. Few men would have been as patient as Ralph; he'd given devotion and in return received—nothing. Practically nothing, anyhow. He was right, too, it was a great strain.

She jumped up and looked in the mirror.

When he'd said that she was jumpy and edgy, it had hurt; it hurt now. She studied her face, the face of an attractive woman of thirty-eight. Of course, she didn't look like a girl, there were a few lines on her forehead and in the corners of her eyes, but—she didn't look old. Did she? There were two streaks of gray in her dark hair, and she would not have her hair dyed. Was she foolish? Had Ralph really meant that she was losing her looks?

No, he'd just meant what he had said, she was edgy under the strain of it. She couldn't go on. He wanted her to tell Wilfred, had been begging her to, for nearly two years. Only Dennis had stopped her. Ralph hadn't much money, otherwise he would probably have been more insistent. Money!

Dennis would probably begin to notice that things were wrong. He was old for his years; too old.

She turned away from the mirror and went to the front door, but there was no sign of the car.

Probably it was a good thing that this had happened when George and Mary, the servants, were out. They would be out all night; they'd taken the job on condition that they could leave after lunch on Wednesday and not return until after breakfast

15

on Thursday; they were such excellent workers that it would have been folly to complain. Usually she enjoyed the greater freedom in the house; and Wednesday afternoons were often *the* afternoons of the week.

Ralph—

She shivered, because it was cold, and went back to the fire.

It was twenty minutes to twelve.

The fire was low, and Muriel put several logs on and watched them blaze, cracking and sparking. Usually they would have been on much earlier; Wilfred would rub his hands in front of them and say, "There's nothing like a log fire, Mew," at least three times. In some moods, she would be at screaming point. She felt calmer than she had before, perhaps because it was nearly time to call the police. She would wait until midnight, now. She relaxed and lay back in her chair, her eyes half closed and the firelight softening—and then she heard a sound in the hall.

She jumped up.

"Wilfred!"

There was no answer. She went to the door and opened it, hurrying into the dark passage.

"Wilf—" she began, and her voice trailed off.

The light from her room showed a man standing by the foot of the stairs, with the front door closed behind him. He had a gun in his gloved hand, a scarf over his face, a trilby hat pulled low over his eyes.

"Good evening, Mrs. Arlen," he said in a hard voice.

She didn't speak. The gun and the scarf made him a sinister figure. The gun, pointing at her breast, didn't move. She found herself breathing hard.

"What—what do you want?"

"You needn't worry," said the man. "I won't hurt you if you do as you're told. Where does Mr. Arlen keep his safe?"

He spoke in a low-pitched voice, harsh and menacing; not natural. She couldn't see his eyes clearly. He didn't move.

"Well, where does he?"

"Why—" she hesitated. "Why should I tell you?"

"Because I'm at the business end of the gun," said the stranger. "And I'm in a hurry, Mrs. Arlen. I wouldn't have worried you, but you've got good ears. Almost as if you were listening for someone!" That sounded like a sneer. "What about that safe?"

"It—it's upstairs."

If she had the nerve, she could turn and rush into the morning room and slam the door on him; then call the police. The man would have to run; certainly he couldn't do her any harm. But she had come too far, she wouldn't have time to get back before he could shoot, and—she believed he would shoot. She just stood there, praying that he would turn toward the stairs.

"Just show me where," he said.

"I—"

"You argue too much, Mrs. Arlen. I wouldn't *object* to shooting you. Then your children would be motherless, wouldn't they? Poor kids!" He backed a few feet, so that there was room for her to pass between him and the stairs. "Lead the way, lady."

She found it hard to put one foot before the other, and it took an age to reach the stairs. She stared at him, but could see only a little of his cheeks and forehead. As she held on to the corner

17

post and turned to mount the stairs he moved forward and pushed her shoulder.

"Don't waste time!"

She made herself hurry up the stairs, and heard him following, although he moved softly. The gun would be pointing at her back. There was nowhere to give security on the gloomy, spacious landing. She was terrified now. She knew that if she screamed he might shoot, and she must keep command of herself.

And—a scream would wake Dennis.

Could she—fool the man?

"If you give me any trouble," he said, "I'll shoot you in the back."

She closed her eyes for a second, then led the way to the door of Wilfred's study. She thrust it open and stepped forward into pitch darkness.

"Stop!"

She stopped dead.

"Put on the light," the man ordered.

She put on the light.

"Now go into the middle of the room, and don't turn round until I say so."

She took a long time to reach the middle of the small room, a study-*cum*-library—Wilfred's "little den." Books lined the wall, a big desk was in the window, there were two armchairs, light oak paneling.

"Go to the safe," the man ordered.

It was in a corner, encased in an oak cabinet. She drew within a yard of it.

"It's—locked," she said.

"Open it," he ordered, and something dropped on the floor just in front of her; Wilfred's key case. She raised her hands, and half turned, in sudden realization.

18

"You've got his—"

The man stepped forward and struck her on the side of the head with his gun. Her head whirled, she staggered back, and he struck her again.

3

Call to the Yard

The telephone bell rang in Roger West's Chelsea home, and he stretched out his hand for it. His wife, sitting on a pouf in front of the dying fire, shook her head slowly and deliberately, moved forward, and put her hand on the instrument before he could lift it.

"No," she said.

"Yes," said West.

"Emphatically, no. You aren't in, darling." Her eyes were filled with laughter. "Try it, this once."

"Impossible. It's half past twelve."

"Darling, *you're* impossible." She pulled the receiver away and put it to her ear, and her eyes mocked West; she was gay and happy. "Hallo, who is that?"

"Scotland Yard speaking. Is Chief Inspector West there, please?"

"I'm afraid he isn't," said Janet in a sweet voice. "He's out with his wife, and I think they'll be *very* late."

"Do you know where they are, please?"

"I'm afraid not," said Janet.

"I see, Miss. Will you ask Mr. West to call the Yard as soon as he comes in?"

"Oh, I *will!*" said Janet, and put the receiver back. "I don't think! See how easy it is, darling? You're too soft. They always ring you first because they know you'll turn out at all hours; now they'll have to find someone else."

She leaned forward, looking up into his face. She was slightly flushed from the fire, her dark hair tumbled to her shoulders in unruly waves, she wore a dressing gown, waisted and with padded shoulders—a gay flowered creation, open at the neck. She also wore a pale-blue nightdress. The mischief was still in her eyes.

"Won't they?" she insisted.

"And I shall be reported in the morning for not being on call," said Roger lazily.

"As if that matters. Take me to bed, darling."

"Later." West leaned forward and kissed the tip of her nose. He was a handsome man in the late thirties, fair-haired, gray-eyed, and looking younger than his years, absurdly young to be a Chief Inspector. "For this, you will dial Whitehall 1212 and tell them that I've just come in, and—"

"Never," said Janet.

"Now," insisted Roger.

"*I'm* going to bed," said Janet, stifled a yawn, and stood up. "I—"

Roger jumped up, caught her in a bear hug that left her breathless, then took her right wrist and placed her hand on the telephone. He stood with his arm round her, and their cheeks were close together. She laughed, and picked up the telephone. He let her go.

21

"Monster," she said. "Darling, how many years is it before you can retire?"

"About fifteen."

"Can't you resign and get a *real* job?"

"I'm not fitted for real jobs."

"Once a policeman always a policeman," said Janet, and suddenly frowned. "All right, sweet, I'll be good." She dialed the Yard. "Hallo?... Someone called Mr. West just now; he's come back."

Roger took the telephone.

"West here."

"Inspector Sloan would like a word with you, sir," said the operator, "if you'll please hold on."

"Who is it?" asked Janet.

"Bill Sloan."

"*He* ought to know better," said Janet. "Darling, do you honestly like being called out at midnight?"

"I love it," said Roger. "Life's long dream... Hallo, Bill?"

He listened.

Janet watched him, saw his faint smile disappear, a frown replace it. He was absurdly handsome and absurdly precious to her, and of late he had seldom been called out at night. She couldn't complain. And Sloan wouldn't call him unless it were urgent.

He said: "Yes, I'll go round."

He put down the receiver, and Janet made a face, but stopped when she saw his expression.

"Is it bad?"

"Nasty. A woman attacked and knocked about, her small son found her. Not far from here, either —Merrick Street. I'll be back as soon as I can."

When he'd gone Janet locked and bolted all the doors and made a tour of the windows.

*   *   *

A policeman on duty outside Number 7 Merrick Street saluted Roger West. The front door was open, light shone out, several people were near the gate. Another constable was in the porch. Men were talking upstairs. Roger hurried up, and saw the tall, bulky form of Detective Inspector Bill Sloan, the portly figure of Malby, a police surgeon, at the foot of a bed. He went into the big, well-furnished bedroom with twin beds. A woman lay on one, with her head bandaged, her eyes open and very bright.

"Don't question her again tonight," the police surgeon said. He was an ugly man, with broad features and full lips, bushy gray eyebrows and a habit of closing one eye. "I've sent for a nurse."

Roger grunted.

"She's given me chapter and verse," Sloan said.

"Description?"

"Not much good. A tallish, lean man."

"Listen," said Malby. "You can talk about this in the other room."

The woman lay staring blankly at Roger, but did not seem to be interested in him. She was easy on the eye. Her face wasn't injured, and Malby wouldn't allow her to stay here if she were seriously hurt.

Roger turned and went out, and Malby said: "There's one thing about you, Roger; you will take a hint. The woman's worried out of her wits—was before this happened. And she might collapse under pressure. I must be off; I need some sleep."

He bustled down the stairs, and Sloan led the way into the study.

Here, three men were working, two looking for

23

fingerprints, one sitting at a desk with some rough drawings in front of him; drawings of the position in which the woman had been found. Sloan talked briskly. The child, Dennis, who was now with neighbors, had been restless, waked up and called for his mother and, not hearing her reply, had gone to find her. He'd seen her lying unconscious in front of the safe, bleeding from a wound in the head. He'd run, screaming, and neighbors had heard him.

"What time?" asked Roger.

"Just after twelve—I didn't lose any, calling you."

"Good. What's the family's name?"

"Arlen."

"Husband?"

"It's a funny business," Sloan said. "She says he is usually home by eight; she was going to call us at midnight, but the burglar arrived just before. He had Arlen's keys, and threw them at her, told her to open the safe. Then he hit her. I've a call out for the husband and his car—a New Austin Sheerline. Arlen is the southern sales representative for the Spark Engineering Company—doing very well, obviously. He covers London and the south, never stays away at night without giving her warning, and seldom stays away anywhere. He was so regular that she began to feel worried when he was an hour late, but didn't care to call us. She says he must have been held up on the road and his keys stolen."

"Could be." Roger fingered his chin. "Where was he today?"

"Brighton, Horsham and Guildford."

"Sheerlines aren't two a penny," Roger said.

"Oh, we'll find it."

"Anything found here?"

"No dabs," said Sloan. "The man wore gloves. He couldn't have been here more than twenty minutes, but cleared the safe out."

"Much there?"

"Several thousand pounds' worth of her jewels, and some money—she doesn't know how much, but not a great deal."

"And Malby says she was worried out of her wits," said Roger thoughtfully.

"About her husband, of course."

"Because he was an hour or two late?"

"Well, if he was usually prompt—"

"Forget it," said Roger. "Did she tell anyone else about Arlen being late?"

"She hasn't said so. I started to ask her, and Malby broke in."

"There's time," said Roger, heavily.

The telephone bell rang. There was an instrument on the desk, and as Roger went to it, Sloan said: "There's an extension downstairs."

Roger picked this one up. "Hallo."

There was a pause, and then a man said: "Is that—is Mrs. Arlen there?"

"Who is that, please?"

There was another pause, before the man asked abruptly: "Are you the police?"

"Yes."

"Oh, lord!"

The man rang off.

The fact that the burglar had Arlen's keys was the one unusual factor. Roger refused to jump to the obvious conclusion, but arranged for a special watch to be kept on the roads. He had finished at Merrick Street by half past two, and by then Mrs.

25

Arlen was sleeping under a drug given her by her own doctor, who had arrived soon after Roger. The nurse—a policewoman—was with her. Neighbors volunteered the information that the servants were seldom in on Wednesday nights; confirmed that it was exceptional for Arlen to be home late.

By three o'clock Roger was back at Bell Street.

Janet was asleep; she didn't stir until he got into bed beside her, then gave a little satisfied grunt and went straight off to sleep again. He didn't go off quickly. He hadn't seen the child Dennis, but whenever a child was involved, he was on edge. His own two boys, Scoopy and Richard, were sleeping in their small rooms; when children were affected, the man as well as the policeman was touched. Arlen might have been attacked and robbed, or might simply have been careless with his keys. Nothing Roger yet knew suggested that Arlen was careless by nature.

Everything was in hand; he went over the routine in his mind.

By the morning details of the stolen jewels would be circulated. All the Home Counties police were alerted for Arlen and the car. He would get a report on Arlen's movements on the previous day as soon as he reached the office; a visit to his employers would be one of the early jobs. The discovering of apparently unrelated facts, the vast mass of information which was mostly unimportant but would conceal a few things that mattered—oh, it was well in hand. There was nothing to keep him awake, but he couldn't sleep.

It wasn't often a case began to prey on his mind so early.

The telephone, at his bedside, woke raucously to life and also roused him. He blinked. Janet wasn't by his side. The boys were talking gaily, and it was broad daylight. He heard the door open and Janet come in, saying: "Why *must* they call now?" He stretched out his hand for the telephone, but she took it first, and wasn't playing this time.

"Mrs. West speaking."

Roger watched her. She hadn't been up long, and still looked sleepy and untidy. Her face was pale, because she had on no make-up. The massive figure of Martin, called Scoopy, then nearly seven, stood in the doorway, watching her, a thumb at his mouth; the habit was almost incurable. Richard, more than a head shorter and much slighter, was trailing behind Scoopy, blue eyes looking huge. They were both of an age when they were realizing the significance of the fact that their father was a detective.

Janet said: "Yes, he's here."

She gave Roger the receiver, and turned to shoo the boys out. They scurried off, staring over their shoulders, and she closed the door and went across to the kettle, now singing on the gas ring in the fireplace.

It was Detective Inspector Evans, of the Yard.

"They've found Arlen's body," he said.

4

Bad News

Roger reached Merrick Street a little after twelve, was admitted by a policeman, and approached by a small, wiry man—an anxious man, who came from the back of the house.

He stopped when he saw Roger.

"I hoped it was Mr. Arlen," he said. "Who—"

"Chief Inspector West," said Roger. "You're one of the staff here, are you?"

"George Rickett, sir. Me and my wife look after Mr. and Mrs. Arlen. Is there any news?"

Roger said: "Not yet." The door was still open, and a tall man wearing a raincoat and a dilapidated trilby stood near the porch; a man with remarkable ears and a vivid imagination, the star crime reporter of the *Daily Echo*. "Close the door, will you?"

The constable began to close it.

"Anything for me, Handsome?" called out the newspaperman.

"Later," Roger waved, and the door closed.

"It's a terrible thing to have happened," said Rickett. He had a pale face, a thin neck with prominent veins, and a long, pointed nose. "My wife's very upset by it, Mr. West. To think it happened when we were out. She says it's my fault, we oughtn't to have slept out; but *we* didn't know Mr. Arlen wasn't coming home, did we?"

"No," said Roger. "Tell her not to worry." He turned to the policeman as Rickett moved off. "Who else is here, officer?"

"Nurse Deacon, sir, still with Mrs. Arlen."

"Go and tell her I want a word with her, will you?"

Roger followed the constable upstairs, and waited in the doorway of the study. The desk chair was facing the door, behind the desk. Instead of seeing it empty, he tried to imagine it as it would have been had Arlen been sitting there. A rather plump, biggish man with a round face, well-brushed curly fair hair, dressed in dark gray. Roger knew what he looked like because of the photographs he'd seen here, not because he had been able to get a clear picture of the face of the corpse. There had been two shots, fired at close quarters.

The nurse, tall and bony, came out quickly.

"Is Mrs. Arlen all right to leave for a few minutes?"

"Oh, yes, sir."

"No relatives turned up yet?"

"The nearest are at Newbury and St. Albans. They're not here yet."

"Friends?"

"Several have inquired, but I said the doctor had ordered complete rest."

"Good. Has she said anything?"

"*Very* little," said Nurse Deacon. "It's a bit funny, sir."

"How?"

29

"It's not easy to explain," said the nurse, whose face was tanned, as if she had just come off holiday. She had keen, intelligent gray eyes; her dark hair was pushed rigidly beneath her nurse's cap. "She's very worried."

"How?"

"I'd say that she *fears* the worst, sir. Almost as if she knew. I don't want to make too much of it, but she isn't ill; she should be much more herself by now, but—well, her doctor says it's shock."

"You've seen plenty of shock cases," said Roger.

"It *could* be shock."

"I see," said Roger. "When do you go off duty?"

"Any time now, sir; my relief's due; but I waited to have a word with you."

"Thanks. Make a detailed report and let me have it as quickly as you can, will you?"

He went toward the bedroom, opened the door and stepped quickly inside.

Mrs. Arlen glanced at him, and there was more interest in her expression than he'd seen last night. She was very pale, and her eyes were shadowed now. He closed the door firmly and walked toward her. She watched him closely.

"You're the Chief Inspector, aren't you?" Her voice was faint.

"Yes—my name's West."

"Is there any news?"

It wasn't the first time he'd had to tell a woman he didn't know that her husband was dead; and it wasn't the first time he had wondered, before telling her, whether she already knew, or guessed.

"Some news, Mrs. Arlen. Did you tell anyone else that your husband was late last night?"

"I—"

"Did you?"

30

"No!"

He thought she was lying. She was frightened, and the nurse had been quick to see it; was she frightened of what might be discovered?

"We shall deal with everything in strict confidence, Mrs. Arlen, but we must know the truth." Roger drew nearer the bed. She sat up a little straighter, staring at him; he thought that she already had an intimation of the news he brought. Did she know? "I'm really sorry. I've bad news for you."

Her hands clutched the sheet; she didn't speak.

"We've found your husband," he said.

She closed her eyes, and he thought that she was going to faint; yet he hadn't said that they'd found the body. His manner was enough to unnerve her, but hers wasn't a normal reaction, more that of someone who was frightened.

"Murdered." He flung the word out.

It sounded brutal; he was being brutal. He watched her closely, and saw the way she sat rigid, as if she had been prepared for the blow. She didn't open her eyes for a long time. After a while, the tense way in which she clutched the sheet eased, and she leaned back.

"The murderer obviously stole his keys," Roger said. "Do you know of anyone who would want to kill your husband, Mrs. Arlen?"

She opened her eyes. "No!" She spoke too abruptly, too emphatically, and there was no easing in her fear. It had not been fear of the news she would get, but of something else. "No, of course not! He'd no enemies." When Roger didn't speak, she went on hoarsely: "Why should anyone want to kill him? *Why?* Unless that man—"

31

"Did Mr. Arlen keep anything except jewels and money and his securities in the safe?"

"I don't know."

"Did you know everything about his business life?"

"If—"

"Did you?"

"No!"

"Didn't he talk much about it?"

"No, he said it ought to be kept out of the home, he—"

"So you don't really know if he had any enemies," said Roger.

"No! No, that's it." She was suddenly and wildly anxious to make that point. "I was thinking of his friends—social friends; I don't know his business friends!" She was clutching at a straw, to save herself from the deep waters of fear; the fear that still remained. "It's—dreadful," she said.

"I'm more than sorry to have to tell you about it."

"Was he—in pain?"

"No, it happened very quickly."

"Thank God for that," she said. "He—but *who did it?* Who killed him?"

"That's what we have to find out," Roger said quietly. "Have you friends or relatives to come and help you? Children? I know about Dennis, that's all. You'll need company, Mrs. Arlen."

"I—I've a sister, in Manchester," said Muriel Arlen. "She'll come. I—I'll telephone her. My daughters are at school; they—" She broke off, and caught her breath.

"Tell me the name of the school, and I'll talk to the headmistress," said Roger, now all friendly. "That will save them from discovering it from the newspapers. I'd advise you to let them stay where they are for today, anyhow, and probably until it's all over."

"You're—very kind. They're at Saldean, near Brighton." She closed her eyes again. "Will you—ask my sister to come? She's at . . ."

Roger made notes.

"You're very kind," Mrs. Arlen repeated in a husky voice. "It's so hard to—to understand. I *can't* understand it." She was being too emphatic again. He judged that she was an intelligent woman; and judged, also, that Nurse Deacon had been wrong: she was suffering from shock. It prevented her from being herself; she was showing her fear too easily. And he'd increased the shock; it was a part of his job he didn't much like. He watched her dispassionately, and wondered what secrets she was hiding. "*Will* you—speak to my sister?"

"Yes, of course. And until she arrives, I'll have a nurse—"

"I don't need a nurse!"

"I think you'd better have one for the next few hours," said Roger. "You don't want to overdo it. There's your son to tell."

That went through her, as a knife; he could see the pain in her eyes.

"He must have some suspicion that there's plenty wrong already," Roger said, and the tone of his voice was deceptively mild. "He—"

"You mustn't tell him!"

Roger said: "Oh."

"I'm not being silly; you mustn't, he mustn't be told! He's not strong, his heart—and he was passionately fond—of his father. If it hadn't been for—"

She broke off abruptly, and then turned her face away and began to cry. She sobbed wildly, trying to stifle the sound by burying her face in the pillow.

Roger watched her, still dispassionately, then went to the door. Another police nurse was standing on the landing. "Come in, and bring your notebook," he whispered, and went back to the bedside. There was no slackening in her crying for several minutes, but at last the woman was quiet.

Roger said: "I'm sorry, Mrs. Arlen, but you can't keep news of this kind away from Dennis."

"You must!" she cried.

"The investigation might go on for weeks, we may even have to question him."

"No!" She sat up, and glared at him. Her eyes were red and the lids puffy, her cheeks wet; her lips quivered and her body shook. "No, you wouldn't be so cruel; not Dennis. There's no need to talk to Dennis."

"We won't, if we can avoid it. It all depends on how much we find out without talking to him. Did you tell anyone else that your husband wasn't home last night?"

She didn't answer.

Roger shrugged. "I'm sorry, but we must know."

He wondered if the job were going to be easy. There were indications here of a carefully planned murder, followed by a burglary to cover it up. It wouldn't be the first time that such plans misfired because one of the parties to it hadn't the nerve to go on. She was distraught. Malby was sure she had been worried the night before; the nurse was sure there was something exceptional on her mind. He could see that she was trying to think, was bitterly angry with herself for her collapse, was trying to retain her self-control. Yes, she showed all the signs of guilt.

He said abruptly: "Were you and Mr. Arlen happily married, Mrs. Arlen?"

She almost screamed: "Yes!" and couldn't have said "No" more clearly.

"I see. Mr. Arlen had no friends, close personal friends, whom you didn't know, I suppose?"

"Of course he didn't!" She should have said: "If I didn't know them, how can I tell you?" but she wasn't in a mood for logical thinking, and yet he sensed that once she had command of herself, she would be much more difficult to break down.

"Sure?"

"He wouldn't, he—he had everything he wanted. Everything!"

"That's good," said Roger. "If you've nothing with which to reproach yourself, you'll feel much better. I don't think he had any idea what was going to happen. Well—not a great deal. I should say he was pretty badly scared for a while; he'd stopped to give someone a lift—that's clear—and it happened soon afterward. Was he the kind of man to give a lift to a stranger?"

"He—no. Yes! Yes, he was very kind, he—"

"Did he usually give lifts to strangers on the road?" Roger barked the question.

She didn't answer.

"He'd be much more likely to give a lift to someone he knew, wouldn't he?"

She kept silent.

Roger said: "Whom did you tell last night, Mrs. Arlen? It isn't any use pretending there was no one. I know there was. The sooner I know his name, the sooner everything will be cleared up. Who was it?"

She gasped: "Ralph wouldn't *kill;* he wouldn't *kill.*"

5

Build-up

Roger pulled up outside Scotland Yard, and the tall reporter with the dilapidated hat grinned at him from the steps.

"In a hurry, Handsome?"

"I'm always in a hurry."

"Any crumbs for me?"

"Try the Back Room Inspector," said Roger, and pushed past the newspaperman, who grinned crookedly as he disappeared. West in a hurry always meant a story.

Roger stormed past the sergeant on duty in the cold, bleak hall, was lucky with the lift, and soon reached the second floor. An inspector in a brown suit, with a large stomach and a pointed nose and receding chin—one of nature's less fortunate men—spun round as if caught in a blast.

"What's up, Handsome?"

"See you later, Eddie." Roger turned into his own office, where Sloan was sitting at one of two desks, fair head golden in the sun which shone across the Thames and into the long, narrow room. "Looked after it, Bill?"

"I sent Peel."

"Fine."

Roger slammed the door and hurried—only to pause as he reached another door; a door which even he would not open without tapping. He tapped.

"Come in."

Behind a large glass-topped desk, sitting in a tubular steel armchair, was the Assistant Commissioner. His office was streamlined, and he sat at the desk looking as if he'd just stepped off a farm cart. He wore pale-brown Harris tweeds, and his round face was a browny-red, darker than the tweeds, his iron-gray hair was grizzled, leaving a brown bald patch in the center. He had guileless blue eyes.

"Oh, it's you," he said.

"Good afternoon, sir; I'm glad I've found you in."

"What's the matter?" Sir Guy Chatworth was by nature suspicious, and never more suspicious than of West when he was respectful. "The Arlen job?"

"Yes."

"Well, if you've caught the man, you haven't lost much time. Have you?"

"Not yet, but it's moving nicely." Roger dropped into a chair at a wave of Chatworth's big hand. "Have you seen the report?"

"A sketchy one. I want to know more."

"Arlen was last seen alive by the driver of a lorry as he turned off the main road to Kingston and took the lane."

"Know why he took a slow road?"

"They say—his wife and his business associates —that it was habit. He may have stopped en route; I'm checking that. Two miles along the road he was forced to pull up—braked very sharply. The tire marks on the gravel surface showed he stopped within ten feet or so. From then on he had a passenger on board—I've checked that he wasn't in the habit of giving lifts to strangers, although his wife tried to pretend that he often did. A mile and a half farther on he was in trouble—nearly ran over a girl on a bike. She came a cropper in the hedge, but caught sight of the number plate and went home and told her parents what she thought of road hogs. Not far from there, Arlen turned left. The car was stopped in the middle of the road. There'd been some struggling in the car, judging from the way the banks on either side were damaged. The car stopped near a gate.

"Arlen was probably shot in the car, dragged out and carried through the gateway. He was found just after seven-thirty this morning by a farm laborer, who walked across that field to his cottage, and was going home to breakfast. Some of the contents of his wallet were taken, and everything of value—money, gold watch, cigarette case and lighter and signet ring. The ring was taken off smoothly, nothing vicious about that. The Austin was then driven off toward London, was noticed by several police patrols, but not seen beyond Putney. It hasn't been found."

"How much of this are you guessing?" growled Chatworth.

"It'll stand up to anything," said Roger confidently. "That's one angle. Next, the wife and her story. She was nervous because he was late, telephoned her boy friend, didn't telephone anyone else and, later, was attacked by a man who was masked, whom she says she didn't recognize, and who had Arlen's keys. She wasn't hurt badly—just enough to make it look as if a burglar with no interest in her had done the job. But when she came round, she was scared, and it wasn't because of her husband."

"Still guessing?" Chatworth was in a dour mood.

"No. She didn't take long to break down part of the way. She'd telephoned a Ralph Latimer. She and Latimer have been *friends* for three years—more than friends most of the time, I fancy. He's thirty-one, several years younger than she is, a gay bachelor, showing some signs lately of being less gay. She says she was worried about her husband and called him to ask his advice, but she didn't trouble to call anyone else. I think Latimer himself rang up Merrick Street late last night. I answered the call myself. I'm having Latimer's movements checked, and Latimer himself followed. I'd like a search warrant for his flat, sir."

"Why?"

"He's out now. He has a service flat, so we could get in. I think half an hour there before he returns would save us a lot of trouble."

"Why?"

Roger began to feel impatient.

"Because Latimer may have done the job, and the woman may have been involved. She could have told us a fairy story. It's got every look of a put-up job—a burglary and assault by her boy friend, just to fool us. We shouldn't expect her lover to attack her, should we? You know how crazy a pair can be when they get together to put a husband out of the way. There's no doubt they were gone on each other. A man often called at 7 Merrick Street on Wednesday afternoons. The servants were always out that day and the son, who lives at home, has a music lesson then. Invalid son," he added. "It's a hell of a business."

"Sure this man was Latimer?"

"She says he usually called on Wednesdays, so do neighbors. He didn't come yesterday. The woman's in a pretty bad way, quite distraught."

Chatworth scratched his nose.

"I don't wonder, when you've been at her. You're the oddest mixture of sentiment and ruthlessness I've come across. So you think it's cut and dried?"

"It wouldn't surprise me, and I think we could be sure if we're lucky at Latimer's flat."

"He'd leave everything he stole in his flat, of course," said Chatworth dryly.

"He'd dispose of it pretty quickly, but I'm after his clothes," said Roger. "Bound to be blood on them. He could have destroyed them, but I'd like to be sure."

"Oh, all right," said Chatworth. "Have your search warrant."

Ralph Latimer had a flat in Mayfair, but it wasn't all that it sounded. It was probably the oldest, smallest and dingiest-looking block of brick flats in London's most exclusive residential district. It was in a small road behind Park Lane; there were twenty-nine other flats in the block, all of two rooms. It was run on service lines, and there was a restaurant in the basement, open to the public but mostly used by the tenants.

A venerable man, the caretaker, unlocked the door of Latimer's flat, Number 21 on the third floor, mumbling protests.

"Thanks," said Roger. "You can go now."

"Even if you are the police, you've no right—"

"You've seen my search warrant," Roger said. "I'm in a hurry."

The caretaker shuffled off. At the entrance,

where he acted as porter by day, were two plain-clothes policemen who would make sure that he didn't warn Latimer.

Roger closed the door as Detective Sergeant Peel, who was with him, stepped in. Peel and Sloan were much alike, big, fair men with fresh complexions and blue eyes; and they had much in common—including clear minds and a habit of independent thought not always popular at the Yard. Peel was in fact slimmer and slightly shorter than Sloan.

"Not much to search, anyway," he said.

A small square lobby, with hooks on one wall for coats and a door opposite, led to the bathroom and kitchenette. Another door, opposite the front entrance, led to a living room; beyond that was the bedroom. Inside, the furnishings and the appointments were better than they had promised outside; without being luxurious, they were comfortable and good. It was obviously a man's flat.

On a piano in one corner of the living room was a photograph of Muriel Arlen, another of a youthful-looking, rather handsome man.

"She's not bad looking," said Peel, who hadn't yet seen her. "I wonder if that's Latimer."

"I wonder," said Roger. "You run through this room. He might be fool enough to have left the gun here, or some of the things he stole. If there's any money, we want it; we may be able to check the notes Arlen had with him."

He strode into the bedroom, where a large single bed stood against one wall with a lamp on a little table beside it. Wardrobe and chest of drawers were big and of good quality.

Roger went to the wardrobe. There were four

42

suits; one navy blue, the others of various shades of gray. He took them down one after another, and felt them for signs of dampness, took them to the window and studied them closely, and saw nothing to suggest that the suits had been washed. There were no stains; and Arlen had bled freely. He found two overcoats and a raincoat; there were no stains on them. He studied the five pairs of shoes, all of them freshly cleaned; there was nothing to suggest to the naked eye that they'd been used for a walk in the country. A magnifying glass revealed nothing, either on the clothes or the shoes. Roger looked in a wall cupboard, under the bed and through every drawer, but found nothing of interest. He felt the first loss of buoyancy as he went back into the other room.

"Anything?" Peel looked up from a corner cupboard.

Roger shook his head.

"Nothing here, either," said Peel, "unless you call that anything." He touched a photograph album which was lying closed on top of a table. "He had plenty of girl friends."

"So I gathered," said Roger. "Pity."

"Why?"

"Because if he were flitting from one to another, he wouldn't want to marry Mrs. Arlen sufficiently to kill her husband for the privilege."

"I suppose not," said Peel. "He did himself proud—half a dozen bottles of whisky, a pretty good general cellar. There are a few oddments in the larder. There's a drawer over there with some lipstick and face powder, all the usual cosmetic stuff."

"Any clothes in the kitchen?"

"No—nothing in the boiler, either; I had a look

43

there. No gun, no gold cigarette case anywhere. A gold wrist watch and two or three sets of gold cuff links in a drawer, that's all."

"Hum," grunted Roger. He opened the photograph album, and the first page had a large photograph stuck in, of a young girl in an abbreviated bathing dress, posing, enticing; a pretty little thing. "Where'd you find this?"

"In that drawer." Peel pointed to a drawer in the corner cupboard. "Locked," he added. "I didn't have any trouble in forcing it."

"Hmm."

Roger turned the page, and was faced by another girl; different in face and costume, but there was no more swim suit here than in the previous one. Next was a head and shoulders portrait; then two more sun-bathing beauties. He ran through them, counting; there were fourteen, but Mrs. Arlen wasn't in this pretty collection. Most of the photographs were signed with a Christian name, and Roger studied the ink. All looked as if they had been written some time ago; he could have that tested and find out if any were recent signatures.

"Just a man with a lot of pin-up girls," Peel sniffed.

"Meaning, not a man to love so deeply that he'd kill," said Roger. "I wonder if I'm right."

"It's early yet." Peel looked up. "Someone's coming," he said, and they listened as footsteps approached along the passage. There was only one other flat beyond this one. It was impossible to judge whether the footsteps had passed, but after a moment or two Peel shrugged and said quietly: "Wrong address."

The front doorbell rang.

"*Right* address," said Roger, swiftly. "Not Latimer; he'd have a key. Keep out of sight, will you?"

He went to the lobby and opened the door slowly, so that he could take a good look at the caller. The footsteps had warned him to expect a woman.

She wasn't much more than a girl.

She was hatless, nice to look at, well-dressed—and worried. Her frown faded when she saw a man she didn't know, and she backed away a pace.

"Good afternoon," said Roger. "Can I help you?"

"Is—is Ral—I mean, is Mr. Latimer in?"

"I'm afraid not," said Roger.

She looked away from him, as if nervously, took a step toward the end of the passage, then quite suddenly jumped forward, pushed past him and ran into the room.

6

Poor Peel

Roger went after her.

As she reached the living-room door, that of the kitchenette swung slowly to, and there was a crash; Peel had knocked something off the table. The girl flew into the room, flung the door back, and cried: "You beast!"

Roger didn't see how it started, just caught a glimpse of the girl disappearing behind the door, with her hand raised. When he reached it, she was striking at Peel, who was crouching as if he had been trying to get into a low cupboard. He defended himself ineffectually as the girl slapped him across the head and punched when his nose showed. When Roger caught her shoulder, she flung him off.

"You cowardly brute!" she cried, and leaped again.

Peel, straightening up, his eyes watering, flung up an arm to defend himself. She thrust it aside and hit him on the nose. Then Roger gripped both her shoulders and forced her away. She struggled, but didn't kick.

46

Peel gasped: "Keep her off!"

"She's all right now."

"She's dangerous! Why, I—"

Peel stopped, staring at her. She no longer struggled, but had become rigid. Roger didn't relax his grip, was prepared for any trick; but this wasn't a trick. Peel straightened up, and wiped his running eyes.

"It's—not—him," the girl sighed.

"Is that how you treat your boy friends?" asked Roger mildly.

"Boy friend! He—" She broke off. "Who are you? What are doing in his flat? Why was he hiding?"

"We'll ask the questions," said Roger, and released her. "Don't go on the loose again, or I'll clap the handcuffs on you." He was only half in jest. "Who are you and who did you come to see?"

"Ralph Latimer, of course; he—" She broke off again, and flung her hands up. "It can't be!" she gasped. "I haven't come to the wrong flat. I—no! I asked for him, and you said he wasn't in."

"He isn't in."

"Oh, *hell!*" said the girl. "What a fool I've made of myself!" She looked about her desperately, and Roger stood between her and the door. She went to a kitchen chair and sat down. "Are you—policemen?"

"What makes you think so?"

"I thought you might have caught up on him."

"What's he done, to let us?"

"If you don't know, how should I?" she asked, becoming wary.

She was in the early twenties, Roger judged. She looked good, although still flushed from the battle. Her hair was untidy, and it suited her that way.

She had a nice figure and was tall for a girl. She stuck her legs out in front of her, slim, well-shaped and sheathed in nylons; and she wore a neat pair of shoes which made one want to glance at her ankles again.

She began to laugh half-heartedly.

"My friend doesn't think it's so funny," Roger said. "You could be charged with assault."

That stopped her laughter, but sudden alarm eased when she saw Roger's expression. Peel, who had been bathing his eyes, turned round, still dabbing at them. She had scratched his nose, and it was bleeding a little at the tip.

"That's right," he growled. "Common assault."

"I didn't mean—"

Roger glanced at him, as if to say: "Ease off." Peel, still disgruntled, dabbed at his eyes again, and took out cigarettes.

"*Are* you policemen?" the girl asked.

"Yes." Roger showed his card.

"Chief Inspector West? *The* West?"

"Just a policeman," Roger said. "Who are you?"

She raised her hands again, stifled a laugh, then drew in a deep breath. He didn't expect what came.

"I'm Georgina Sharp—Gina for short, soft G; I'm twenty-four; I'm an artist's model and like it; this is the first time I've committed a crime, I *think*, and I came to tell Ralph Latimer exactly what I thought of him."

"And what do you think of him?"

"That he's a rat!"

"Let you down?"

"Let *me* down? I wouldn't let the Ralph Latimers of this world get within a yard of me. He's poisonous. I told Meg so as soon as—"

48

She broke off.

"Meg?"

"Meg's a—er—Meg's a friend of mine," said Georgina Sharp, weakly.

"You're better at telling the truth," said Roger. "Even if you don't tell us, we can find it in half an hour. Who is Meg?"

"My—sister. But she doesn't know I've come; she—"

"You're protecting your little sister's good name, are you?"

"Little? She's older than I, and hates anyone to know she's made such a fool of herself. I only forced it out of her because she's been so funny lately—couldn't sleep, always got a headache and brooding. I knew it was a man. She always goes like that when a man's let her down; she can't hold them, somehow; but this time—the brute—"

"What did the brute do?"

Georgina Sharp looked suddenly wise and very young.

"I don't *have* to tell you. It might be slanderous, and I'm not going into any police court, nor is Meg. It would just about finish her off. I think—think I want to see a solicitor."

Roger laughed.

Peel, unexpectedly, chuckled, and moved across to the girl.

"I've forgiven you," he said. "Like a cigarette?"

"Oh, thanks!"

Roger gave her a light.

"Do policemen always behave like this?" she asked. "I shall expect to be offered a cup of tea next. Or is it only when they want to get something out of—er—a person?"

"That's right; we're full of deep cunning," said

49

Roger. "Whatever you think Mr. Latimer has done to your sister, you can tell us in confidence. We shan't let you down, and—"

"Oh, no," she said sarcastically. "If I made a charge against him and you wanted to prove it, you wouldn't make Meg and me go into the witness box, would you? I'm not *that* young. I *do* want to see a solicitor," she added firmly. "That is if you're going to ask any more questions."

"Let's see," said Roger. "Where do you live?"

"Kensington."

"In the gutter, or a shop doorway?"

She put her head on one side.

"You're quite a wit, aren't you? I live at 122 Middleton Street, Kensington, which is near Barkers, and I share a top-floor flat with Meg. It's a hole, really; but we do the best we can with it. Meg's wonderful with a few odds and ends of materials."

"And you're an artist's model?"

"If you don't mind."

"*I* don't mind. How long have you known Latimer?"

"On and off for years, but it's only lately that I've got to know him well."

"And Meg?"

"Oh, she's been going with him for about a year, I think. She—" The girl paused, and bit her lip. Now that she had recovered from her outburst, she looked candid and attractive. To his eternal credit, Peel was watching her with amusement, and at the same time keeping an eye on the door. "Listen, Mr. West—or do I call you Chief Inspector?"

"Mister will do."

"If I do tell you, will you have to take any action?"

"I might."

"And would you need Meg as a witness?"

"If I knew what you were talking about, I could tell you. If it could be done, I'd put up other witnesses, to avoid causing anyone distress."

"And anything I said would be in confidence?"

"Safe and sound."

"The brute's been fleecing her," said Georgina abruptly. "Nearly five hundred pounds. That's a fortune, for us. He promised to pay her back a hundred; last night he was to have come to the flat. *I* was there waiting for him. But he didn't turn up."

"Perhaps he knew you were waiting," said Peel.

"That's nothing to do with it."

"And you suggest this was theft," said Roger mildly.

"Of course it was!"

"Did she lend it to him?"

"She lent him some, but he stole the rest."

"Sure?"

"Meg says so, and Meg doesn't lie to me."

"I see. It could be argued that if she'd lent him some he took the other in good faith, I suppose," said Roger, with a blank expression. "On the face of it, it's not a charge; but it might become one. Nothing worse?"

"If you don't think five hundred pounds of my sav—"

Roger looked into the pretty, startled face, as she broke off.

"So it was *your* money."

"Well—"

"Did you lend it to Meg?"

"I—it—no! Oh, forget it!"

"Don't be silly," said Roger.

"I'm a complete fool," declared Georgina Sharp, forlornly. "I ought to have kept my silly mouth shut. Meg always said I talk too much. It was *our* money, really; we have a joint account."

"And Meg forgot to tell you how much she was drawing out, and when you discovered it, told you the truth," said Roger. "What time were you expecting Mr. Latimer last night?"

"Seven o'clock."

"How long did you wait for him?"

"All the evening."

"And he didn't show up at all?"

"I don't think for one moment he intended to," said the girl. "I don't think I ever did, but Meg was sure he would. In spite of everything, she still thinks he's wonderful—but weak. She—is—quite impossible. Sometimes I wonder how we ever came to be sisters. But you don't want to be worried by my troubles or Meg's. I wonder if you could—er—just *suggest* to the brute that if he doesn't repay the money, there will be trouble."

"I'll think about it," said Roger. "Do you know any of his other friends?"

"A few," she said carelessly. "He gathers women to him as moths to an electric light. You see how modern I am!" She was being facetious to cover up her nervousness. "He's quite an Adonis, if you like them dark and languorous."

"*I'm* not dark," Peel said.

"I just saw a man hiding—anyhow, your arms hid your head," she said defensively.

"I'm not languorous, either."

She laughed. "He's not, always. When I first met him I thought he was quite something. I couldn't believe that Meg was on to a good thing at last—and wasn't I right!"

She glanced round and saw the man's photograph, next to Mrs. Arlen's.

"Is that him?" asked Roger.

"Yes. Look here, why were you here?"

"Waiting for him."

"How did you get in?"

"We had authority. I shouldn't worry about that. Will you do something for us, Miss Sharp?"

Her eyes were round and guileless.

"Will it get Ralph in trouble?"

"It might."

"He may be a heel, but I don't have to be," she said.

"You'd never know, and all you'll do is to save us a little time," said Roger. "Go home, and write down the names of his friends—with their addresses, if you know them—and the places he usually goes to. Where he takes your sister out to dinner, for instance."

"She takes him out," sniffed Georgina. "Yes, I'll do that; I can't see that it will do any harm, but—I won't tell Meg. I don't want to upset her, and she's upset enough as it is. Do you have to come and collect the list?"

"Bring it to me, at Scotland Yard."

"Love us," said Georgina. "Me at Scotland Yard! Oh, well, you've been pretty nice about it all. I'll see what I can do. Of course, Meg knows more about his friends than I do, but I can probably squeeze some tidbits out of her. May I go now?"

"Yes."

She stood up, and turned to Peel.

"I am really sorry about that nose," she said. "I couldn't see you properly, it's dark in that corner, and I thought you—he—was hiding from me, and I just—"

53

"Think no more of it," said Peel, handsomely.

"Thanks. Fancy policemen being human beings," said Georgina.

She shook hands gravely with each of them, turned and went out, without looking round. They let her open the front door herself.

It had hardly closed before Roger said:

"After her."

"Right!" said Peel, who was already on the move. "Mind you, I shall keep my distance."

He grinned, and went out cautiously, then closed the door.

7

Search for Latimer

Peel had left a pile of books on the table in the
living room. There was an address book, bank
statements, other books which showed that Latimer was a contact man for several small firms in
the West End—introducing business which varied
from jewelry to cosmetics, furs to gowns and hats
and a variety of other commodities. He lived on
the commissions, and apparently lived fairly well.
The bank statements showed nothing of unusual
interest; he had a few hundred pounds to his
credit.

Roger sat at the table and ran through the address book. There were many entries, both of men
and women. Against some, always women, were
little red dots. There were seventeen of these.

Roger stretched out for the photograph album.

There were fourteen photographs in it, and nine
were signed with Christian names which coincided
with the Christian names of the marked women.
There was no one named Sharp, and Mrs. Arlen
wasn't in the address book.

He made copious notes, put back everything as

he had found it, went through the clothes again and satisfied himself that nothing was blood-stained and nothing had been washed or cleaned. He didn't think it would be worth having a more thorough examination of the clothes at this stage. He had been here over an hour and a quarter, and but for the intervention of Georgina Sharp, it would have been ordinary dull routine; the kind of routine which sometimes led to results, but was seldom spectacular.

He put the album under his coat, took the photograph of Latimer from the frame, and went out.

The caretaker-porter was sitting in a little cubbyhole in a corner of the hall, and the detectives were sunning themselves at the entrance.

They smartened up as Roger appeared.

"One of you stay here," Roger said. "Don't speak to Latimer if he comes in, and telephone me at once."

"Right, sir!"

"The other come with me." Roger went to his car.

Nothing had come in at the Yard. Sloan was out. Roger studied Latimer's photograph, and wondered why women found him so attractive. He was a dark-haired man with a long jaw, good-looking in a heavy, languorous kind of way. He sent it to the Photographic Division, to have copies made, and went through the names and addresses of the seventeen young women. He sent a list of these to Records and fifteen minutes later was called on the telephone.

"Bray, here," said the Inspector in charge of Records.

"Anything?"

"Care to come over?"

"All right," said Roger, hopefully.

Records was a room of shelves and filing cabinets, a library of known criminals. Bray, big and plump and nearly bald, sat at a small desk with his back to a large window. He had a button of a nose and a loose mouth, and talked as if he were eating plums.

"Siddown, Handsome. Not much here, but one or two int'resting things. See." He pointed to three photographs, smaller than those from the album, but obviously of three of the women. "There's Elizabeth Morris, up twice for taking drugs, had a six-months cure last year, haven't heard anything about her since. Spiteful nature, see that—clawed the skin off a man's nose once."

Roger grinned.

"What's funny?" asked Bray, who was not renowned for his sense of humor. "Then there's Lilian Brown. Remember her? Of course you don't; no memory, some of you people. Lil got twelve months for helping old Corry the Con. Wonder what's happened to Corry; haven't heard anything of him since he came out. Never a big cheese; how anyone ever fell for his spiel I could never understand. Talk about a fool born every minute! Pretty as a picture, Lil was; nice kid gone wrong. Then there's Maude Pepper; got twelve months for running a disorderly house. At twenty-three, mind you! She was a hard case, Maude was. Haven't had any reports on her since she come out, either."

"I'll have them all checked. Anything else?"

"No."

"Nothing about the Sharp women?"

"Not at that address, and not those Christian names," said Bray. "You can't tell; lies run off their tongues sometimes. You know that."

"Latimer?" asked Roger.

"Nope."

"All right, thanks. Let me have the report, and I'll get busy on them."

He went to the office of Superintendent Abbot, his immediate superior, and spent five minutes with him—a satisfactory five minutes, because he was given full charge of the case.

Sloan was in the office when Roger got back, writing a report in his bold, schoolboyish hand; he still tucked his tongue into the corner of his mouth when he was concentrating on a report, and at such times looked almost foolish, blond and brainless. There were few shrewder men at the Yard. He glanced up but didn't stop until he had finished a sentence and made a full stop with great deliberation.

"Latimer went out at half past twelve last night, and didn't come back," he announced.

"Sure?"

"Yes. There's no porter on duty after nine-thirty, but a man in the next-door flat saw him go. He'd been out from five o'clock to about nine, that's certain—and that's all we know about him. He may have been out between half past nine or so and midnight, and come back just for a wash and brush-up! He hasn't been in any of his usual places today. I've been taking it easy, and haven't given anything to the press, but—"

"Don't yet," said Roger. "But put some more men on the job. Any one of these women might know where he is."

He gave Sloan the album.

Sloan glanced through it.

"Phe-ew!"

"He's an eye for a pretty face," said Roger. "I

couldn't find anything on his clothes; on the other hand, he wasn't around at the time that matters. We've a photograph of him now; better have it sent round to all stations and mark it not for public release."

"Right."

"Nothing in about the bullets in Arlen's head?"

"Not yet," said Sloan.

"I'm going up to Ballistics," Roger said.

Scrymegour, in charge of the Ballistics Department, was an unusual man for a London policeman; he was short and thin. He sat between rows of rifles, automatics and revolvers of all shapes and sizes, which lined the walls. A bench near the window was equipped with a microscope and several other instruments—mysterious to most people, simple to Scrymegour. He was writing in a swift, flowing hand, and on the desk were two bullets, each with a piece of thin string tied round them and with a small label attached.

"Arlen job?" asked Roger.

"Always in a hurry, that's your trouble," said Scrymegour. "Yes. These are .32s, probably a Smith & Wesson; but you can say I'm guessing and you'll be right. The bullets were fired at close quarters—you've seen these, haven't you?"

"These" were photographs of Arlen, after death.

Scrymegour pointed with a pencil.

"Singe marks on the temple and cheek, big blast opening inside the head; I'd say that they were fired within a couple of inches. Each would have been fatal; but you've had the medical report on that, I expect. Usual marks on the bullets; but we've never had any with the same marks before —unknown gun. Find us the gun, and we'll prove these were fired from it, though."

"I know you will," said Roger. "Well, if that's the best you can do, I'll be off."

He nodded and disappeared, before Scrymegour could make a comeback. But he wasn't feeling particularly bright.

He went to the Assistant Commissioner's office. Chatworth was out, and that made him feel brighter.

It was nearly five o'clock.

He checked that the only prints found at 7 Merrick Street were those of Arlen, his wife, Dennis and the servants; the thief hadn't left any, and that made the thief pretty smart. Was Latimer smart? True, any little crook knew the danger of leaving prints and could protect himself against doing so, but usually there were some traces. The attack at Merrick Street and the assault in the car suggested a man of strong personality who knew exactly what he was doing—that was if they could take Mrs. Arlen's story at its face value.

He'd call in and see her again on his way home.

He drove to Middleton Street from the Yard. Kensington High Street was crammed with people and with traffic, crowds were disappearing into the station in droves. He turned left and then right and came upon Middleton Street. A few people were walking along, but there was no sign of Peel.

This was a street of tall, narrow houses, built in terraces; not the best type of Kensington property. Many of the houses had APARTMENT notice boards up, and 122 was one of these.

Peel wasn't in sight.

Roger parked his car near 122, and entered the house. The front door was open, as was often the case in apartment houses. There was a notice board, with cards pinned onto it, and at the top was a card reading: MISS MARGARET SHARP, MISS GEORGINA SHARP. The card was curling at the edges and yellowing with age; they'd been there for some time. He went up narrow, carpeted stairs to a gloomy landing. The three doors were each fitted with Yale locks. Someone came into the house behind him, but stopped on the ground floor. He reached the third and top floor, where there was only one door—also fitted with a Yale.

He rang the bell, and there was an immediate answer.

A woman, tall, big-breasted, wearing a navy-blue dress, looked at him inquiringly. He couldn't see any likeness to Georgina, who was a race horse to this cart horse. But that wasn't quite fair. The woman was magnificently proportioned, her dark hair was braided, and she had bold, handsome looks. Her eyes were dark.

"Good evening."

"Good evening," said Roger. "Are you Miss Margaret Sharp?"

"Yes, who—"

"I wonder if you can spare me a minute," said Roger, and slipped past her. She was too surprised to try to stop him. He beamed at her and closed the door, then led the way into a room beyond this small hallway.

It was much larger than he had expected, long and narrow, with tall windows. It had the charm of home-made furnishings, with a restful color scheme of blues and grays. A baby grand piano stood in one corner, there were a divan and several easy chairs; the boards were polished and rugs were dotted about. Daffodils stood in tall vases on the piano, the window ledges and the mantelpiece; an electric fire was on.

"Really!" exclaimed Meg Sharp. "You've no right—"

"I'm a police officer."

Roger still beamed, and showed his card.

She gasped: "Police!"

"Yes. I believe you're a friend of Mr. Ralph Latimer."

"*Ralph*," she sighed.

"Yes—Ralph Latimer. Has he been here today?"

"He—no. No! You—you *want* him?"

"I'd like to have a word with him," said Roger. "Nothing that need worry you, Miss Sharp, but I think he can help us."

"He—he's not in trouble?"

She stood facing the window, and he could see the lines at the corners of her eyes and her lips; she was not far short of forty.

"Why should he be in trouble?"

"You—you're a *police*man."

"We have to talk to a lot of people who aren't in trouble," said Roger. "How long have you known Mr. Latimer?"

"About—about a year," said Meg Sharp slowly. "Oh, this is so worrying. He was to have come to see me last night, and didn't arrive. I was sure that something was the matter; he *wouldn't* let me down. Not *Ralph!* I—oh, no! No, no, no! He hasn't been—*hurt*."

She stretched out a hand, almost touching Roger's, and her eyes glowed with alarm. He could understand what her sister had meant about Margaret Sharp.

"Oh, I don't think so," said Roger. "When did you see him last?"

"Friday," said the woman promptly; it had obviously been on her mind. "Friday, we went out to

62

dinner. I thought he was worried; he—he wasn't having any luck, you know; he's the most unlucky man I've ever come across. Oh, I do wish you'd tell me what's the matter."

"I just want to talk to him," said Roger easily. "I'm sorry to hear about his bad luck. Betting, you mean?"

"Oh, *no*. Ralph isn't a betting man; it's just that his business deals won't go through; someone always stopped him. I tried to help him as much as I could. Oh, poor Ralph! I—" She broke off, only to breathe: "No!"

Her sister must find her trying on occasions.

"No!" she repeated. "Gina wouldn't—Gina! She —that's my sister—she's just left; she's been asking questions about Ralph's friends; she—*have you seen my sister?*"

"I had a few words with her."

"No!" cried Margaret Sharp. "It's too wicked. Too, too *wicked*. Gina—Gina hasn't told you anything?"

"About what?"

"I can't believe she would let me *down*," gasped Margaret. "Anyhow, she's wrong! I lent him the money; it isn't true that Ralph stole it. I tell you it isn't true; I lent it to him. If anyone did anything wrong it was me. I didn't tell Gina that I was taking so much out of the account, but it was a joint account; it wasn't a crime. And I'd do anything for Ralph, anything. He's—wonderful! I'll never forgive Gina, never; she—"

"We wanted to have a word with Mr. Latimer before we saw your sister," said Roger soothingly. "I shouldn't blame her—but if Mr. Latimer comes here, you'll ask him to let me know, won't you? Here's my card." He put it on the table, but she didn't look at it, stood in the middle of the room with her hands clasped in front of her massive bosom, like a prima donna about to break into song. "Good evening, Miss Sharp."

Roger was at the door before she had turned round. He closed the outer door with a bang, but didn't latch it; after a moment, he pushed the door open and crept to the door of the big room.

The woman was standing where he had left her, looking out of the window, with tears falling slowly down her cheeks.

Sloan was in the office, at Roger's desk, and looked up eagerly as Roger came in. It was nearly half past six.

"We're moving," he said abruptly. "That Austin's been found. It was in a builder's yard at Hammersmith—not damaged. Coming?"

"Am I!" They went out of the office together. "What else?" asked Roger.

"Not much. The builder is a small one, who buys secondhand cars occasionally. He wasn't in to business today; the workmen at the yard thought this was a new buy, and didn't say anything about it. A bright constable passed the yard and took the number—I didn't get word until ten minutes before you came in."

They reached the main hall of the Yard.

Peel and Georgina Sharp were walking up the steps, smiling and cheerful, and Peel had a helping hand on the girl's elbow.

8

Dusk

Mr. Lionel Bennett, at sixty-three, was a happy man. He had all the prerequisites of contentment, for he was wealthy, he played golf with a handicap of five, and a surprisingly agile game of tennis. He had a pleasant house on the outskirts of St. Albans and—because of his remarkable foresight twenty-two years ago, when he had married a woman fifteen years younger than himself—he had the satisfaction of knowing that he was going home to a comely and attractive wife who studied his whims and fancies, and who would always be a source of pride as well as comfort.

He had reached the summit of his ambitions three years ago. Then he had retired and been asked to name his own parting gift from his company—of which he had been a loyal and successful servant for nearly forty years. He had dared to suggest a dream, a substantial dream, in the shape of a Rolls Royce.

He had always longed for a Rolls Royce, because he believed that it would set the crown on his worldly success. He told himself that he did not really value worldly success; he was a regular churchgoer, and subscribed with reasonable generosity to many charities and good-will organizations. He was also a Mason.

Moreover, he had two sons, one aged sixteen and the other aged eighteen, who were already proving a credit to him; the elder was almost certain to get his cricket Blue at Cambridge when he went up; and to make sure that Mr. Bennett's joys were evenly spread, his younger son was showing promise as a brilliant mathematician; quite exceptional, Bennett had been assured.

That evening, as dusk fell, he strolled from the clubhouse of his golf club, a few miles from his home, and stood for a moment admiring the lovely lines of the Rolls Royce. If anyone had told him that he was in love with it, he would have laughed, and said "Nonsense"; yet the look in his eyes was very like the look which he had bent upon his wife twenty years ago.

Stanway, the club secretary, came out of his office.

"Like a lift, George?" asked Bennett.

"No, thanks, I'm not quite finished," said Stanway.

"Oh, well, if you're sure." Bennett moved toward the car. "Everyone else is busy; I have to be home at eight sharp tonight. Sir Henry Cuff is dining with us."

"Oh, really," said Stanway. "Good night, old man."

Bennett sat at the wheel, fiddled with the instruments, listened with delighted ear to the soft purr of the engine as the self-starter worked; this was the perfect machine. He took her out of the main gates and then turned along the road which led to the main road and, soon, his home.

It was a narrow, winding road, and because he was by nature careful, and also because the slightest scratch on the shiny black surface appeared to him as a major tragedy, Bennett drove with great care. Although it was not really dark enough for them, he switched on his headlamps; at the sharper corners he made the deep, trumpetlike horn sound. He handled the car, in fact, as if it were a precious toy, and had been doing that for over two years.

He turned a corner slowly.

Out of the hedge at the side sprang a man—tall, dark. He stood in the middle of the road, quite still. Bennett jammed on his brakes; the Rolls Royce had seldom been called upon to stop so suddenly.

"You crazy fool!" He felt the blood rush to his head in anger. "Get out of my way!" He put his finger on the horn, and the note blared out. "Get out of my way!"

The man moved, but kept a hand on the car. Bennett released the hand brake, but couldn't move without risking injury to the man. Suddenly, the other sprang to the door farther from Bennett, opened it and got into the car.

"What the devil do you mean? Get out!"

"You're not very polite," said the stranger, in a deep, sardonic voice. "You're going to give me a nice ride."

"I'm damned well not! Get out, or I'll push you out."

"Well, well, what vigor for an old man!" said the stranger, and put his left hand to his pocket—a movement which Bennett did not notice. "Drive on."

Bennett put on his hand brake again. "Get out!" He was almost incoherent with rage. "Get out before I—"

"Before you what?" asked the stranger, and showed his gun.

Bennett gaped.

The gun rested on the stranger's knee, pointing toward the dashboard. The car was wide enough for there to be plenty of room between driver and passenger, and Bennett couldn't get at the gun, even if he'd had the impulse. He felt shivery; and shivered more violently when the stranger gave a little laugh. Bennett saw his face only vaguely.

"Let's go," said the stranger.

Bennett muttered: "What—what do you want? I haven't any money with me—not much; I—"

"Never mind that. I want a nice ride. Turn right at the next corner; you know the road, don't you?"

"I—I have an urgent appointment at home, I can't be too long."

"They'll wait for you, won't they?" asked the stranger. "You've a nice little wife. What a lucky man you are! Have you ever realized that? What a *very* lucky man, with your lovely home and your family—"

"Do—you know me?"

"Perhaps I'm just guessing. Isn't it time you started to drive?"

Bennett moistened his lips, then let in the clutch. The car moved off slowly. The road to the right was half a mile farther along. He didn't want to take it. He couldn't safely put on speed along this lane; oncoming traffic was often careless here, and there were sometimes cyclists. His mouth was dry, but the shivering fit had passed. He was not without physical courage, but was getting on in years. He thought of grappling with the man, who looked strong.

The gun still showed.

The grass verge and the hedge showed up in the headlamps, and the signpost appeared; the right-hand turn led to a hamlet several miles away, and to one or two isolated farmhouses.

He slowed down.

"You've remembered," said the man with the gun. "That's good. Be careful you don't scratch your fenders, won't you?"

Bennett gulped.

"I—I've fifteen pounds in my pocket, take that and—"

"But I don't want your fifteen pounds," said the stranger. "At least, that's not all I want. You're a happy man, aren't you, Mr. Bennett? You've led a good life. A *very* good life."

The sneer was all too evident.

"I—I've done everything I could to help others. I wouldn't mind helping you, if you'd tell me what you want."

He had turned the corner. Here the hedges were high and the road narrower. It was much darker. The young leaves of hawthorn and bramble showed up pale in the light, and here and there a tall tree was thrown up in dark relief. A few stars now powdered the sky, and the red light of an aircraft moved overhead.

"So you've done everything you could to help others," said the stranger. "And you've got yourself a plump little wife and two children and a fine home, haven't you? You've retired on a big income

69

and you've plenty of money—everything you need in life."

"I—I get along."

"What a fine understatement!" said the stranger. "You get along! You'll get along all right, Mr. Bennett." He leaned forward, and Bennett slowed down. "Be very careful, and look at me."

Bennett obeyed. The man's lips were parted, and his eyes were glowing; they looked as if there were fire in them, in spite of the gloom. Bennett started violently, the car swerved and scraped along the hedge.

The stranger moved the wheel, to steady it.

"So you've recognized me, *Mister* Bennett! I thought you would. Slow down and then stop—gently, or my gun might go off."

Bennett obeyed, but his hands were shaking. The car stopped.

"Listen! I—I'll give you everything I have; take my watch, my cigarette case, my wallet, take anything!"

"But I don't think it's enough."

"Let's go home; I've some money in the safe, some jewels, too; you can have those. There are several thousand pounds' worth; I—"

"If I let you take me home, you'll find a way to call the police," said the stranger, "and I should hate that. Look at me, Bennett."

Bennett looked at him.

He didn't see the gun move; only the flash followed by the deafening report.

"But it's so unlike him," said Mrs. Bennett to Sir Henry Cuff, who was a self-important and most influential man. "I've never known it happen before.

70

Sometimes he's late at the clubhouse, but when we have guests he's most punctilious."

"An accident, no doubt, an accident." Cuff drew on his cigarette. "Don't worry, my dear Mrs. Bennett. It will be a trifling affair, trifling. What a charming place you have here—so charming!"

"I'm glad you like it," said Mrs. Bennett eagerly. "It's always nice to hear what others think. Lionel's so fond of it."

"Lionel is a very lucky man," said Cuff, and patted her arm.

He was plump and red-faced, and had little hair; there was a faint sheen of perspiration on his upper lip, for the room was warm. A bright fire roared, the central heating had been turned on at full blast. They were in the drawing-room, overlooking the garden, which was now hidden by the night. A Knole suite of pale blue and gold, smaller chairs to match, draped velvet curtains—everything here was expensive and in excellent taste.

Mrs. Bennett was short and fluffy, pink and white; her hair was hennaed to gingery blond, like a young girl's. She had on a little too much makeup, especially rouge. Her excellent teeth showed a great deal as she smiled. She couldn't keep still, and kept shifting her chair, looking round toward the door, behind her, and obviously listening for the sound she longed to hear.

"I just *can't* understand it," she said. "I'll telephone the clubhouse again; *do* forgive me."

The telephone was in a corner of the room. She stood by it, dress billowing, well corseted, a comfortable bundle of a woman who paid the proper attention to foundations. Cuff sat back on the couch and watched her in the concealed wall lighting, admiring her movements.

71

"Hallo!—is that Mr. Stanway? Oh, Mr. Stanway, are you *sure* my husband has left? He's not home yet; it's Mrs. Bennett here....*Could* there have been a mistake?"

She listened.

"Oh, dear," she said plaintively. "Well, thank you very much."

She replaced the receiver slowly and reluctantly.

"He left at seven; he should have been home at half past; that would have given him good time. I *can't* understand it. Do you think I ought to telephone the police?"

"My dear lady, if it will ease your mind, of course, of course. Allow *me* to speak to them," said Cuff, in manly fashion, and stood up. When he reached her, he patted her shoulder. "It will prove to be a trifling delay, trifling, and I am in no hurry."

"You're *very* good. Thank you so much. And there's dinner, it'll spoil. I—I'll go and see cook."

She hurried out.

"No, sir, there's been no report of any accident," said a man at the St. Albans Police Station. "No, nothing at all tonight...a Rolls Royce, driven by Mr. Lionel Bennett...Mr. *Lionel* Bennett!...We'll keep a lookout, sir, and let you know if there's any report....Yes, sir, I'll let Mrs. Bennett know."

For Mrs. Bennett it had been a miserable dinner. She hardly noticed that her companion did full justice to Dover sole and roast lamb.

They were back in the drawing room.

"My dear lady, I can't leave you in such distress, I really can't." Cuff fingered his watch; it was nearly ten o'clock. "I *really* can't."

He was a widower.

"Oh, but you'll be so late, and you didn't come to see me; you came to see Lionel."

"I have been delighted to spend the time with *you*, Mrs. Bennett. The problem is, what to *do*? What to *do*? The police would surely have informed us had there been any accident, have no doubt of that. He must have been—ah—he must have been—ah—"

"It's so *unlike* him. He wouldn't go off like this, if he could help it. I—I must speak to the police again."

"Allow me," said Cuff.

"No, sir, there's been no word. I think we'd better put a call out and have the movements of the car traced.... Yes, sir, I'll call you the moment we have any news."

It was an unusual situation. Of course, there was the staff, three in all; but they were at the back of the house. Cuff sat in an easy chair in one of the spare bedrooms, the best spare room at Hillbrae, with a whisky-and-soda by his side. He was undoubtedly doing the right thing; no one worthy of the name man could leave the little woman alone. The problem was whether he was doing everything he could and should to ease her mind.

It was a *remarkable* situation.

He knew Lionel Bennett well. Was it possible that he was a dark horse, and—no! No, that was absurd. True, he might be a dark horse where the ladies were concerned, and no one would blame him for that, but he wouldn't select tonight as an occasion for a peccadillo. Bennett had a proper respect for others, had always admired success, and

73

certainly there were few more successful men in England than Sir Henry Cuff. Was it, perhaps, amnesia? That *could* happen—it was worrying, especially worrying for Mrs. Bennett. Sweet and charming little woman; it was a thousand pities that he hadn't been able to see her at her best. Had Bennett telephoned to say that he would be late, for instance, she would have resigned herself to an evening in his company, and they would have enjoyed it; undoubtedly, enjoyed it.

He glanced at his watch; it was five minutes to twelve.

He had loosened his collar and shoes, but was fully dressed. The room was pleasant and warm—not so warm as it had been downstairs, but happily anxiety had prevented Mrs. Bennett from thinking of the fire, which had died low later in the evening. She must be—distracted. She *must* be. Would it—would it be discreet to go and see her? She would be in bed by now, probably; or perhaps she was restless and hadn't yet undressed. There was surely no harm in going to her door and finding out what was happening.

He stood up, fastened his collar, smoothed down his hair, cleared the corners of his eyes, and turned to the door. Then he realized that his shoes were undone, and glanced down at them; it would be better to do them up properly. He bent down with an effort, and the blood went to his head; as he straightened up, he was quite giddy. That soon passed, and he went toward the door, remembering the room into which Mrs. Bennett had gone; the one on the right. Next to it was her husband's study, where, had things gone according to plan, he and Bennett would have talked over port and cigars.

He opened the door.

A man, wearing a trilby hat and with a scarf over his face, was coming out of the study.

Cuff opened his mouth in an O of astonishment.

The man moved his right hand.

There was a flash and a roar....

9

Coincidence

Roger looked up from the kitchen table, where he was having breakfast, and Scoopy came in from the garden, cheeks flushed, short, straight hair untidy, a smear on the side of his nose. He looked very solemn. Richard, wearing a school cap back to front, came running after him.

"No, Scoopy, no!"

"Daddy—" began Scoopy.

"No, I've got to ask him!" cried Richard. "You said I could. It's not fair."

"Daddy-could-you-take-us-out-to-tea-this-after-noon?" The request came out with a rush from Scoopy.

"*I* wanted to ask you," cried Richard. "It's not fair, I hate—"

"Could you, Daddy?"

Scoopy was wide-eyed with hope.

"Did you tell Richard he could ask?" asked Roger.

"No, I—"

"Oo, you did! You wicked liar, you did! You—"

"Easy on the language," Roger said sharply.

"Well, he *is* a liar."

"Oo, I'm not," denied Scoopy. "I thought of it first."

"You *didn't!*" Richard's eyes were very blue and bright whenever he was angry, and his cheeks flushed. "*I* thought of it first. I hate Scoopy!"

He punched Scoopy on the shoulder, and it had not the slightest effect.

"Richard—"

Janet was hurrying downstairs.

"What on earth's the matter? Scoopy! Richard! Stop fighting. Stop it!" She came hurrying in, and muttered beneath her breath. "You're hopeless; I can't leave them to you for ten minutes without something like this. Scoopy! Richard!"

The boys stopped fighting, but glared at each other.

The telephone bell rang.

"I'll go," said Roger, and hurried out, dabbing at his lips. He grinned as Janet proceeded with a scolding, and the boys stood mute. He turned into the front room, and the telephone was still ringing. "Hallo!"

"Roger?" It was Bill Sloan.

"Yes."

"Get here as soon as you can," said Sloan. "There's been a second Arlen job."

"Those St. Albans people were quick," said Bill Sloan. "They found one of the two bullets in Bennett's head, close to the surface, and it's up with Scrymmy now. He can probably give us a report. If those bullets don't tie up with the couple we took out of Arlen's head, I'll eat my hat."

"Don't risk your hat," said Roger.

They were in his office.

"St. Albans saw the similarity between this job and Arlen's and the Hertfordshire Chief didn't lose any time asking if we'd help," Sloan went on. "It's an almost identical case, except that they found the body earlier. Mrs. Bennett gave the alarm, there was a special watch, and they found out the road that the Rolls had taken. It was discovered—"

"What was? The Rolls?"

"Sorry, no—Bennett's body—the car's gone. Bennett was discovered behind a hedge by a constable who'd been told to keep a sharp lookout. That was just after one o'clock. Half an hour earlier there'd been a report of a burglary at the Bennets' house; Sir Henry Cuff was shot—and died before he could speak."

"What was he doing there?"

Sloan told him what he knew.

"And Bennett's wife?"

"She heard the shot and came rushing out, and saw the man disappearing through the front door. He'd been in the room next to hers, and hadn't made a sound. The safe in the study had been opened with keys—and Bennett's keys were missing. About two hundred pounds, several thousand pounds' worth of jewelry and a few other oddments were taken."

"How much have you put in hand?" asked Roger.

"Not much. Peel's trying to find out if Bennett and Arlen were associated, of course. St. Albans are doing the preliminary work."

"Latimer?"

"Still missing."

"Anything to indicate that Mrs. Bennett really knew anything about it?"

"I wouldn't say that," said Sloan, "but apparently she was wide awake; yet says she didn't hear a sound. The house is well carpeted; St. Albans say that it's possible. The killer let himself into the house with a key, of course—the job's almost a carbon copy of what happened at Arlen's."

"Let's go and see Scrymmy," said Roger.

The little ballistics expert was standing at his bench, examining two bullets between the special double microscope. He didn't look up, but kept turning a small wheel. The others saw that he had cut two bullets into two, longways; two halves were on the bench, the others under the instrument. He stood with his back to Roger and Sloan for several minutes, then straightened up with a hand at the small of his back.

"This lumbago," he muttered. "I'll have to lie up for a day or two." He moved, and almost fell. "Oh, it's you, is it?"

"Bad luck, old chap," said Roger.

"A fat lot you care. Well, you ought to be happy."

"Same gun?" cried Sloan.

"Take a look."

There were two lenses; Sloan and Roger took one each. Roger fiddled with the wheel. The two halves of the bullet were gradually brought together; there were differences on the markings, but some looked very much alike. After a few minutes, the main markings, which showed in lines, matched up; these looked like two halves of the same bullet.

Roger drew back and picked up the other halves. One was labeled. "Arlen" and the other "Bennett."

"Your hat's safe," he said to Sloan. "Three killings, same man. The nurse told me that Arlen has relatives at Newbury and St. Albans. Find out if the lives of any of the three victims crossed, and that's urgent. Maybe there's a family vendetta."

Chatworth was at his desk, and looked up at Roger sourly, like a farmer surveying a field of ripe corn after a high wind and heavy rain. Roger put a bundle of papers on the desk and stood waiting. Chatworth shook his head slowly, and said: "Oh, sit down."

"Thanks. The same gun was used."

"You didn't ever think it was a coincidence, did you?"

"It wasn't likely," said Roger. "Latimer's still missing."

"With his bloodstained clothes, I suppose," said Chatworth sardonically. "You jumped at Latimer too quickly. Now you can't find him. Why?"

"He walked out of his flat about half past twelve that night and hasn't been seen since. We've questioned most of his girl friends, and not one says she saw him. Most can prove they were with someone else. Three can't, and I'm checking further. Two I haven't found. There's no sign that anyone's lying."

"Any more of them give money to Latimer?"

"Three," said Roger.

"What about the Sharp women?"

"They seem straightforward. The older one, Margaret, was in love with Latimer—there isn't much doubt about that. I'm having them watched; Peel's on the job."

"Why?"

"If Latimer runs short of money, he's as likely to try the Sharps as anyone."

"If Latimer did these jobs, he isn't going to run short of money very soon."

Roger shrugged.

"Well, is he?" barked Chatworth.

"I doubt if he'll get rid of those jewels easily; they're much too hot. He's collected a bit of money in cash, but we have the numbers of most of the notes, which were new. He'll see that, and be careful. A list of the note numbers has been circulated, of course."

"What else?"

"I'm going down to St. Albans," Roger said. "And I want to find out if any one of the three dead men knew each other. Sloan's on that. The only other thing—"

"Yes?"

"I think we ought to give the press Latimer's photograph. Warn the public that he's wanted for questioning after the two hold-ups. If we hold the murder picture any longer and there's another tonight or in the next day or two, they'll scream blue murder at us. We don't want another mess of that sort, do we?"

"Never mind what the press will say about us; will it help if the papers have that photograph?"

"I think so."

"All right, give it to them. Got one here?"

Roger opened his file and selected the picture of Latimer that he had taken from the flat. It was full face. Chatworth studied it for a long time, and then looked up.

"What do you make of it?"

"It's a long time since I started guessing from photographs," said Roger.

"You're too fresh," growled Chatworth. "The man has a weak face—hasn't he? His reputation is in line with it—sponging on different women, living on them, in effect. Is he the kind of man you'd expect to run around killing motorists?"

"Could be," said Roger. "There isn't much risk to

himself, the way he does it; but if everyone is on the lookout there should be some risk. I'll give it to the press, then."

"Yes, go ahead," said Chatworth.

Roger closed the door softly. Chatworth wasn't in a good mood, and there was no particular reason for that, unless it were a personal one. Roger went back to his office and lifted the telephone.

"Yes, sir."

"See if you can get me Wycherly of the *Daily Echo*," Roger said, "don't let anyone know it's the Yard."

"Right, sir."

"So you're releasing the photograph," said Sloan.

"I'm beginning to think we were a day too late," said Roger.

He fiddled with his cigarette case, waiting for the bell to ring. It still hadn't rung when there was a tap at the door, and Peel came in.

Roger looked at him without enthusiasm.

"Morning," said Peel.

"Why have you deserted Georgina Sharp?" asked Roger. "Tired of holding hands?"

Peel stared—and then colored. His reaction was so startling that Roger forgot his impatience, and Sloan widened his eyes. Peel looked as if he were biting his lips to keep back a sharp retort, then relaxed and said formally: "She's working. I've left a man to watch the place where she is, but she's usually there all day."

"Who's the artist?" asked Roger.

"William Fell."

"I never could understand a girl wanting to sit in the altogether while a chap paints her," said Sloan, scratching his head with a pencil. "I suppose these artist chaps do get impersonal, but I wouldn't like a daughter of mine to take up that job."

"Wouldn't you?" asked Peel, stonily.

The telephone bell rang.

"Hold on a minute, Peel," said Roger, and lifted the receiver. "Thanks . . ."

He waited for a few seconds, and the voice of the tall and untidy reporter of the *Echo* came.

"Who wants me?"

"I do. It's West. If you happen to be at the Back Room in about twenty minutes, you might get something interesting," said Roger. "It'll be your own fault if you don't get there pretty quickly. Follow?"

"Well, well, a present from a policeman," said Wycherly. "Could I ask the great Handsome West what he expects to get out of it?"

"A lot of space on the front page of the *Evening Echo*," said Roger. "Good-by."

He looked up into Peel's eyes as he finished. Peel seemed to have recovered his poise, and was standing at ease. Roger offered cigarettes, and said easily: "I've a feeling we're going to have some night work for the next week, Peel. Get some rest this afternoon, will you, and be here at about six o'clock? You'll probably have to keep at the Sharp women. I've also a feeling Latimer might try to get some more money out of them."

"Right-ho." Peel was brisk. "I can manage night and day for a bit, if—"

"Not on a job where there's a killer with a gun," said Roger. "I'm going to ease up for a few hours myself. Was Meg Sharp at the flat when you left?"

"Yes—it's watched."

"Thanks," said Roger.

Peel went out, and Sloan said: "Well, well! He

hasn't developed a soft spot for the little lady, has he?"

"We'll find out," said Roger. "I hope he doesn't start mixing romance and work, but—no, Peel won't fall for that."

"Meaning?"

"If Georgina Sharp knows more than she's told us, she might think it a bright idea to have a friendly policeman," said Roger. "I'll have a go at him myself, later on. Now I'm going out to see Mrs. Bennett."

Mrs. Bennett was prostrate, and her doctor forbade questioning. Roger went through the papers in the study, checked with the St. Albans police, but found nothing of interest.

While he was there, the Yard telephoned a report that the Rolls Royce had been found, parked behind some trees in the garden of an empty house at Hampstead. The only fingerprints were Bennett's.

It was three o'clock before Roger reached Chelsea, and he didn't go straight home. He telephoned the Yard from a call box, was told there was nothing fresh to report, and then drove to Merrick Street. There was now only one policeman on duty, in the garden. A young, serious-looking woman— Mrs. Arlen's sister—met him in the drawing room. Yes, Muriel could see him; she was in her room but much better, and was actually sitting up. She'd just pop upstairs and warn her—

"Do you mind not doing that?" Roger turned. "Thanks. I know the way."

He knew that the sister was standing and watching him as he went upstairs, but didn't look back.

He tapped on the bedroom door, and Mrs. Arlen called: "Come in."

She was sitting in a chair in front of a gas fire, wearing a blue dressing gown. She hadn't made up, but her hair was neat, she was quite attractive —and still frightened. At sight of him, she started. He closed the door softly, and strolled across to her.

"I'm glad you're better, Mrs. Arlen, and sorry I have to worry you again. It isn't much, but—did your husband know a Mr. Lionel Bennett?"

"Lionel Bennett? Of course," said Muriel Arlen. "They were cousins."

10

Cousins

"I don't see what's so surprising about it," said
Muriel Arlen. "Why do you ask? If you think that
Lionel had anything to do with—" She broke off.

Roger smiled.

"No, not that. Were they good friends?"

"I suppose you would say so," said Mrs. Arlen.
"They weren't close friends; we only saw Lionel
and Mary about once or twice a year. There wasn't
any quarrel or anything like that. Why?"

"Do you know when they last saw each other?"

"Just before Christmas. We went to their house
near St. Albans."

Roger said: "Did Lionel Bennett know Ralph
Latimer?"

"I can't imagine why you're talking about
Lionel," said Mrs. Arlen in a sharper voice. "Of
course he didn't know Ralph. I've told you the
truth about that. Do you want to humiliate me any
further? Isn't it bad enough—"

"I don't want to humiliate you or anyone," Roger
said gently. "I just want to get at the truth. How is
your son?"

She didn't answer.

"Does he know yet?" asked Roger.

"He—he knows that his father was hurt, that's all. Some neighbors have been looking after him; they've been wonderfully kind. They say that he took the news very well. I ought—I ought to have told him myself, but just couldn't bring myself to it. The whole thing has been—damnable! It would have been bad enough in any circumstances, but to bring Ralph into it—Mr. West, do you *seriously* think he had anything to do with it? Tell me, please. I keep turning it over and over in my mind; I can't get any peace."

"We don't know. We can't find him."

"Can't *find* him? Do you mean he's run away?"

"I don't know. Mrs. Arlen—" Roger went across to her and looked down, wondering what was passing through her mind. He was sure that she was in torment. Her eyes looked heavy, yet bright, as if she had a blinding headache. "Did you ever lend Mr. Latimer any money?"

She started violently.

"So you did," said Roger.

"I—I helped him once or twice! And he invested some money for me. It was mine—not much, but mine; I didn't want—my husband—to handle it. I always told him that I was quite capable of looking after my own affairs."

"How much?"

"I—I'm not sure. About—about two thousand pounds, I suppose."

"Recently?"

"No, not really—six months ago was the last. Mr. West, you must tell me why you're asking all these questions. I must know!"

"You trusted him implicitly, didn't you?"

"Of course I did!"

"I wish you hadn't," said Roger, and was still gentle. "He wasn't worth it."

"You can't mean that; you're lying!"

"I'm afraid not. He's borrowed money from other women."

She gave a little whimpering sound. "Oh, no! No."

There was utter silence in the room. She sat back in her chair, the head resting on the back, staring straight in front of her, as if she were looking into horrors. Roger, letting the news sink in, felt sorry for her, and knew he now had a chance that wouldn't be repeated.

She relaxed.

"He's not worth suffering for, Mrs. Arlen. It was Latimer, wasn't it?"

"No!" she cried. "No, it couldn't have been; Ralph wouldn't have killed. I tell you it wasn't—I *know* it wasn't him. It doesn't matter how you blacken his name; he didn't come here and attack me."

"You couldn't see his face."

She didn't answer.

He tried a shot in the dark.

"Did he paint?"

"Paint? No, of course not. I—I don't believe that he borrowed money from other women. I just don't believe it; you're trying to trick me. And you can't, because I've told you everything I know."

"All right," said Roger quietly.

He went out; and repeated the trick of leaving the door ajar and looking back into the room. Muriel Arlen leaned back in her chair, with her eyes closed, and her expression reminded him vividly of Meg Sharp's.

She was in love with Latimer, she was a handsome woman, and when she wasn't suffering like this, she would be intelligent; a woman of taste, too. Like Meg Sharp. What had Latimer about him to make two such women fall in love with him? They weren't young girls.

They were about the same age, both unhappy and lovely in their different ways; easy meat for a plausible rogue.

Mrs. Arlen's sister was waiting at the foot of the stairs.

"Have you upset her?" she asked abruptly.

"Bad news *will* upset her," said Roger. "How much has she told you?"

"About this man Latimer, you mean? Everything. And it wasn't as bad as you think."

"Sure?"

"I can't imagine why she should lie to me now," said the sister. "I think it's true. She wasn't his mistress in the usual sense. She hoped to get a divorce and remarry, but there was always Dennis."

"Had she ever mentioned Latimer to you before?"

"No. I knew she wasn't happy. Wilfred was an impossible bore. Oh, I know he's dead, but it's true. I can understand what happened. Is Latimer any good?" she asked abruptly.

"No."

"Poor Mew!" said the sister, gently. "I'll go up to her."

"Just a minute," said Roger. "I want a list of your relatives—especially blood relations of Mr. Arlen. Can you help?"

Roger used the telephone in the downstairs room, and talked fast, to Sloan.

"They were cousins. Take down these names and

addresses of other relatives. Have each one warned to be very careful at night. Then start probing—find out if any of these relatives know Latimer."

"Right!" Sloan was brisk.

It was after half past seven when Roger reached home. Richard was singing at the top of his voice, as he often did before going to sleep. Janet was moving about upstairs. She went into one of the rooms, and he heard her say firmly: "You mustn't worry about it, Scoopy. Sit up and read, or do some drawing—you can't always get off to sleep quickly. Good night."

She closed the door with a snap, then came hurrying downstairs. She wore a green dress, her hair was freshly brushed and glossy. Her face brightened at sight of him. He stood at the foot of the stairs, she on the step above, and they kissed lightly.

"Can't Scoopy get off to sleep again?"

"He's having a bad spell, and it's worrying," said Janet. "I suppose he'll be all right."

"I'll pop up—"

"It'll only excite him; leave it for a bit," said Janet. They went into the kitchen, his arm round her waist. "How's the case going?"

"So-so."

"I don't like it much," said Janet. "I've seen the *Evening Echo*. The man can't be sane."

"I'm not so sure," said Roger.

"Have you found him?"

"No. Forget him for an hour; I may get a call any time. Anything for a hungry man?"

"You go and sit down; I'll get supper," Janet said. "You're looking tired already, and it's only just started. What is Mrs. Bennett like?"

"Plump, placid, almost prostrate, according to the local men who've seen her."

Janet shrugged, and frowned.

The evening paper was lying folded on the seat of his chair. He picked it up, dropped into the chair and poured himself a whisky-and-soda; Janet had put the bottle and syphon out. There were pictures of the three murdered men and of the two wives; most of the front page was taken up with the story; Wycherly had used everything. The picture of Latimer was centered, an excellent reproduction of the photograph. By now the Yard was probably getting reports that the man had been seen; there would be a hundred such reports in by midnight; he would have been "recognized" from Land's End to John o' Groats. And not one of the reports could be neglected, in case one might be the one that mattered. Roger sipped his drink, and turned to look out of the window. The half light was full of shadowy gloom.

This was the time when two men had died.

He jumped up, put on the light and made himself think of routine. There would be hundreds of interviews, hundreds of reports, each one to be studied closely; he couldn't leave it to the others. Sloan would go through them first, and Sloan didn't miss much; but unless there was an early clue, he'd have to handle the lot himself. He yawned.

Janet brought the supper tray in.

They'd finished, and were listening to a quiz on the radio when the telephone went.

"Hallo," said Roger, into it.

"We've traced one of the pound notes he stole from Arlen's pockets," said Sloan. "A café in Soho.

I thought you'd like to know. Shall I go, or will you?"

"I'll go," said Roger. "Send Peel round, with all the photographs, will you? I'll meet him there."

It was a dingy side street in Soho, and might have been a thousand miles from the bright lights of Piccadilly Circus and the roar of London's traffic. Near the Café, which was open, was a small and exclusive restaurant. Peel was standing nearby. They met and went into the café, which was near a street lamp so that they could read the sign: SALVATORE'S. Inside, half a dozen men and several girls—obviously foreign, almost as obviously Italian—were sitting at small tables. A red Cinzano sign hung on one wall. A man was eating spaghetti, crouching over the table and gulping it down, digging his fork into the big heap and twisting it round expertly. A little man with a round, oily face and thick dark hair which was combed back from his forehead in deep waves was standing behind a counter. He had a high color, needed a shave, and his brown eyes had a velvety softness.

Roger and Peel stopped at the counter, near the hissing, bubbling coffee urn, and the little Italian behind it smiled at them nervously.

"You *polizia?*"

"Yes," said Roger, and showed his card. "Are you Salvatore?"

"Sure thing—come thissa way, mister." Salvatore opened a flap in the counter; a buxom woman, even shorter than he, took his place by the urn. He led the way into a small back room, crammed with furniture and cardboard boxes. A double bed was in one corner, and there was only just room to stand alongside it. Rickety chairs dotted that space. "Sitta down, pliz," said Salvatore, "I wanta to help da *polizia*."

They sat down.

"About this pound note," Roger said, and Peel took the note from his pocket. "How did you come to give it to the police?"

"Mister?"

Peel said: "His English isn't too good. Two of our men sometimes come in here for a cup of good coffee, and did this evening. They asked him to show them his one-pound notes, and this was among them. It's the only new one of the lot. He said he paid in to the bank this afternoon, and only changed three pound notes up to the time he was questioned."

"*Si, si,* I am da truth," broke in Salvatore. He held up three fingers. "One, two, dree. And thatta one, he was bad man. Ver' bad man; he looked like dis." He scowled and hunched his shoulders, shot out an arm and whipped a trilby hat from a chair, jammed it on his head, pulled it low over his eyes, and glared round. "So! But he was not fat, no. Thin."

"Would you recognize him again?"

Salvatore looked blank.

"Would you know him again?" asked Roger patiently.

"*Si, si, signore!*"

Roger took the photographs, which Peel had in a large envelope, and handed one to Salvatore; the man shook his head. He tried two more, before showing the picture of Latimer. For the first time, Salvatore paused.

Neither of the Yard men prompted him.

"Could be, yes; could be, no," said Salvatore, pursing his lips as he finished. "Yes, no. I dunno!"

He waved his hands. "Could be da man, could not be da man, yes?"

Roger showed three more photographs, and Salvatore brushed them all aside impatiently.

"Was he alone?"

"By himself, yes."

"Had he ever been here before?"

"No, no."

It wasn't worth showing the pictures of the women.

"I am good man, yes?" asked Salvatore hopefully.

"Very good," said Roger. "If that man comes again, give him coffee and food, and tell your wife to telephone Scotland Yard. Or to go and get a policeman. Do you understand?"

"I go myself, personal," said Salvatore proudly.

They walked along the dark street, without speaking. All they had learned was that the murderer had changed one of the notes. There was no certainty that he had been at the café; he could have changed it through a third party. The likeness to Latimer was a long way from conclusive; the line had fizzled out, although the district would be combed for the man.

Peel said: "I hope nothing's happened tonight."

"So you have that feeling, too."

"Couldn't help it," said Peel. "At dusk I was as jumpy as a cat. At least you'd warned all the relatives—Sloan told me about that. Given us a new slant, hasn't it?"

"Rejecting the long arm of coincidence," said Roger, and stopped by his car. "Yes. What have you made of that list of Latimer's known friends?"

"It's fizzled out," said Peel. "Several of them were the girls whose photographs were in that album. There were only three men, and they don't amount to anything. I've seen several of them; Sloan's seen the rest, except for two. All of them can account for their movements, all swear they haven't seen Latimer for a couple of days. The two have changed their addresses, and when I last heard we hadn't found the new ones. Sloan may have them by now. Oh—Georgina Sharp made up a list; none of the names appear on both."

Roger switched on the engine.

"Are you going to tackle the relatives?" Peel asked.

"My job for tomorrow," said Roger. He turned on the police radio set. "Chief Inspector West calling, West calling and standing by."

He lit a cigarette as the response came through in a clear, unhurried voice.

"Stand by, please; there is a message for you. Stand by, please."

Peel said: "Hal-lo!"

The wait seemed a long one. Was it news of a third attack? Had the killer sprung out of the dusk to strike again?

"Calling Chief Inspector West; can you hear me?"

"I can hear."

11

8 Milbury Road

Milbury Road was in the residential part of
Fulham, near the Thames. The street was well
lighted, there were patches of garden surrounded
by low walls in front of every house. Two cars were
drawn up at one corner, two others in a side street.
Sloan was standing round the corner as Roger
pulled up, and he moved forward.

"You haven't lost much time," he said. "I've only
just arrived myself."

"What's the story?"

"We found the address of one of the two girls
who'd moved—Number 8. She has rooms here. We
alerted the district, and received another report
from a man on the beat—that someone roughly
answering Latimer's description was known to
have come here this evening, just after dusk. The
constable kept an eye on the place, and no one's
come out."

"What's the girl's name?"

"Rose Morton—does a bit of dancing, a bit of
singing, gets an occasional leg-show job, and some
night-club work, but she hasn't been working

much lately. The rumor is that she has a man who now looks after her, and it could be Latimer. She's known Latimer for several years."

"Let's go," said Roger.

He climbed out of the car, and Peel got out the other side.

Sloan led the way.

"There's always a chance that he got out the back way, of course. We've had the back covered for the last twenty minutes, but he had plenty of time. There's a service lane—all of these houses have back gardens."

"Go round to the back, Peel, will you?" asked Roger, and Peel hurried off.

Number 8 was near New King's Road, and across the main road they could see cars passing, a bus slowing down, yellow light glowing from its square windows. The house was between street lamps, and the front door was as dark as any in the street. No one but police appeared to be near. There were a few lighted windows, but no light shone at Number 8.

Roger and Soan approached the front door, and stood in a little square porch. Two Yard men were at the gate, a couple of yards behind them. Roger pressed the bell, but there was no response. He pressed again, and knocked; the knocking seemed to reverberate as if this were an empty house.

"Search warrant?" he asked.

"Yes," said Sloan, tapping his pocket.

"Let's try a window."

"Half a minute," said Sloan.

There was a movement inside the house, and a light came on. They stood on either side of the porch, Roger nearer the door. Someone fumbled with bolts and a chain, and then the door opened a few inches.

"Yes, who is it?" The woman's voice was sharp.

"Good evening," said Roger, and placed his foot against the door. "We're police officers. Are you Miss Rose Morton?"

"*Police?*" The door opened wider. She showed dimly, a tall, fair-haired woman. "Did you say you were police?"

"You heard it. Is Mr. Latimer here?"

"Ralph?"

Roger said: "We'll come in, Miss Morton." He pushed the door wider, and she didn't protest. There was a light behind her, on the first landing. Roger saw the dim outline of a light switch on the wall, and pressed it down. Miss Morton, hennaed, tall, good-looking in a hard way, blinked at them. "Is he here, Miss Morton?"

"No, of *course* not!"

"Sure?"

"You've no right to—"

"Mind if we have a look round?" asked Roger. "We've a search warrant."

"You ruddy coppers," she said. Her voice had a common note. "Hounding the lives out of us, that's what you're always doing. No, he's not here; he's gone."

"So he's been here."

"Any reason why a man shouldn't come to see a lady?"

"When did he go?"

"Half an hour ago," said Rose. "You'd better come upstairs." She licked her lips, and turned to the staircase, which was opposite the front door. "My rooms are up here; you don't have to look in the others, it'll only cause trouble."

"Trouble with whom?"

"My landlady—she's out," said Rose Morton. "Gone to the pictures; they always go on Friday nights."

"All right," said Roger, but as she turned to lead the way up the stairs, he signaled to the plainclothes men. They would go through the downstairs rooms, and make sure that Latimer had really left.

The light from the landing actually came from a back room. It was comfortable, but not particularly attractive—a living room with a divan in one corner, and oddments of furniture, none of which matched. Rose had a swaying, attractive walk, and now that they could see her better, she proved to have a good, full figure. She looked sullen.

"Now what's it all about?"

"Why did Latimer come to see you?"

"He's a swine," she said. "He wanted some money—he's always after money. I'd told him I wouldn't have anything more to do with him; my—my *husband* wouldn't like it. I didn't think he knew where I lived, but he turned up tonight. Thank heavens, my *hubby* wasn't in." Having got away with "husband" without being questioned, she seemed much easier. There was a gold ring on her engagement finger. "He said he was pushed for twenty pounds, and I gave him a fiver to get rid of him. It was all I had. I said if he came again I'd have the police on him."

"For what?" asked Roger.

"Never you mind!"

Roger said: "Now listen, Rose. We haven't anything against you; we don't want to make difficulties. If you're settling down and you've got a steady man, that's fine. But we want straight answers about Latimer. Have you seen the evening papers?"

She said: "No. What's he been doing?"

"We're not sure that he's been doing anything yet, but he may be able to help us about the Arlen murder."

"Murder?" To their astonishment, she giggled. "Ralph, a murderer? Don't make me laugh; he hasn't got the guts to punch a man on the nose!" She giggled again. "You've made some mistakes in your time, copper, but not a bigger one than this. Ralph's small cheese. He wouldn't kill; he'd be too scared. He'd put up a good front, but I know him—I know he's got water where most men have blood."

"What do you know about him?"

"He—he peddled snow," said Rose Morton abruptly. "*I* didn't fall for it. Snow and heroin; other dope too, I wouldn't be surprised. I found it out from one of my girl friends, and wild horses wouldn't drag her name out of me, so you needn't waste your time. I told him tonight that if he came again I'd tell the police about it—I don't think he'll come again."

"What made him come?"

"I've told you."

"You haven't told us why he thought he could get money out of you," said Roger.

"He knew I'd settled down, and wouldn't want my hubby to know some of the little games I got up to in the past. He's always putting on the squeeze, if he gets half a chance. But I wasn't having any, and I told him so—after this once, he could tell Fred anything. In fact"—she put her chin up—"I'm going to tell Fred myself. I don't see any point in living under a shadow, and if he's as

ond of me as he says he is, Fred won't mind. I
think he *is*."

"That's fine," said Roger. "You tell him. Did
Latimer say why he wanted the money?"

"He said he had to pay someone back some
money he borrowed."

"Did he tell you he was on the run?"

"No, but it doesn't surprise me—he looked
scared, for once. Usually he covers it up, but he
couldn't cover it tonight. He wasn't here ten minutes."

"Which way did he go out?"

"Why, the front way, of course."

Roger said: "It's no good, Rose; you're lying."

"I'm not; you damned splits never believe
anything!" She glared at him. "He went out the
front—"

She broke off.

"That's right; try second thoughts," said Roger.

"Now I come to think of it, I didn't hear the front
door close," said Rose. "I was so glad to get rid of
him, I told him he could find his own way out, and
slammed the door on him. He could have gone out
the back door; he would if he knew you were after
him, wouldn't he?"

The men who had been searching came into the
room.

"Nothing here," one said.

"Of course there's nothing here," snapped Rose
Morton. "I've told you the truth—he wasn't here
for ten minutes."

"Did he say where he was going?"

"Why should he? No, he didn't."

Roger said: "All right, Rose; but listen. We want
to find Latimer, and if he shows up again, hold
him on some excuse and let us know. Don't let any

101

fool ideas about loyalty stop you, because if you help him get away, you'll find yourself in trouble with us. Your Freddy wouldn't forgive that so easily, would he?"

"Coppers," sneered Rose.

They were back at the Yard at half past nine. There had been no reports of any trouble, and there was no fresh information.

The morning newspapers splashed the murders and the photograph of Latimer. Roger left home just after eight, and by nine was looking at a mass of reports on his desk, all from people who thought they had seen Latimer. He had been in thirty-one places at the same time, according to these. The largest file was in the Metropolitan area; Roger would need to go through those first. He wanted to start on the other angle, the relations of Arlen and Bennett, but he'd have to sift through these first.

He was on edge, half expecting a report of a third attack at any moment. None came.

Sloan was late.

Roger finished going through the reports, marked a dozen for special attention, and left them for Sloan, then pulled the files which covered the relatives toward him. There were four in all; a woman and three men.

The woman was a Mrs. Lilian Drew, and lived on the outskirts of York. Her husband was known to be extremely wealthy, director and chief shareholder of a large chain of grocery stores. Two of her brothers, Arthur and Ernest Bennett, lived in Birmingham. Lionel had been the fourth member of this family—their mother had been an Arlen, sister of Wilfred's father.

The two brothers were the only directors of Bennett Brothers Limited, a small manufacturing company the shares of which were not quoted on the Stock Exchange.

The other man was Raymond Arlen, of Newbury; his father and Wilfred Arlen's had been brothers.

The provincial police had been quick; there were comprehensive reports on all of them. All four were people of the upper middle-class social strata, with good incomes, all married and reputable. Their ages ranged from Arlen's forty-seven to Ernest Bennett's sixty-one. Each had been warned the previous evening, and there was a telephoned report from the local police, saying that nothing had happened to any of them up to 6:00 A.M.

Sloan came in breezily.

"Morning, Roger. Haven't kept you, I hope."

"Oversleep?" asked Roger.

"Good Lord, no! I got the address of that other woman Latimer knew, and paid her an early call on my way. She says she hasn't seen him for months. She's living at Ealing, married and respectable; there's nothing to it. No more trouble, I hope."

"Not yet," said Roger. "I'm going to Birmingham first, I think, and I'll take Peel with me. These Bennetts—"

The telephone bell rang.

Roger took off the receiver. "West here."

"Morning, sir." It was the servant on duty in the hall. "A Mr. Raymond Arlen is here, sir, asking to see you."

12

Raymond Arlen

This Arlen was tall, lean, an obvious open-air type. He came in swiftly, nodded his thanks to the sergeant who had brought him up, and looked from Sloan to West.

"Good morning, Mr. Arlen," said Roger. "I'm Chief Inspector West."

Sloan pushed up a chair.

"Sit down," said Roger. "Cigarette?"

"Thanks." Raymond Arlen seemed completely at ease, and looked curiously round the office. "This is the first time I've been in a police station—if you call Scotland Yard a police station."

"It'll serve," said Roger. "How can I help you?"

"I thought it time I showed up," said Arlen, and smiled. He had fine white teeth, dark hair—he was by far the youngest of the cousins, and showed no sign of going gray. "I had your message last night, of course—kept it to myself; it would have scared the wits out of my wife."

"Better that than have you killed."

"Oh, yes. But is there seriously any risk of that?" asked Arlen. "I don't mind telling you that if anyone has a crack at me, I shall fall back on the law of justifiable homicide."

"So long as you make sure it's justifiable, no one will mind," said Roger easily. "You'd heard about the murder before we telephoned, of course."

"Only just." Arlen drew at his cigarette and blew two smoke rings. "I'd been away for a couple of days, and had missed the newspapers. Couldn't get the *Times*, and I've no use for the scandal sheets. I was reading about it when the telephone rang. My wife had seen it, of course; she was pretty worked up—and that's one of the reasons I've come to see you."

"Yes?"

Arlen said easily: "We're just about to have our first child, Mr. West. It's due in a few weeks' time, and my wife is pretty nervous. You can understand that, can't you? I don't want her worried any more than I can help. So I thought if I came to see you it would save you coming to see me, and perhaps save her a lot of worry. I have to come to town on business quite often; caught an early train this morning—she's no idea that I've come here, of course."

"Thoughtful of you," said Roger. "It's saved me a journey, too. What time did you get home last night?"

"About seven. Soon after."

"And you'd been away for two days?"

"Yes—North Wales. Business, of course. I travel for Willersons, the paper people."

"Your murdered cousins were salesmen, weren't they?"

Arlen grinned.

"If you'd called Lionel or Wilfred a salesman, you'd have come away with a flea in your ear—

they were traveling representatives. Lionel was more than a salesman, anyhow. Yes—that's about the only thing we really had in common—the gift of the gab. It runs like that sometimes."

"Your other cousins don't seem to have it," said Roger. "The Birmingham couple are—"

"They run their own business—small tools," said Arlen. "They can talk all right!" He laughed. "But I haven't cottoned on yet, Mr. West—why should you think that there's any danger for the rest of us? I take it you warned all the lot."

"Yes."

"Well, why?"

Roger said: "On the simple principle that it's better to be safe than sorry. I've no grounds for thinking that the murderer might have a go at you, but the connection is an odd coincidence, isn't it? Have you read this morning's scandal sheets?"

Arlen grinned.

"Every one—I've never seen so many headlines in my life. You mean this chap Latimer."

"Do you know him?"

"Never heard of him."

"Did you recognize him?"

Arlen didn't answer.

Roger said: "Well?"

"As a matter of fact, I had a feeling that I'd seen him before somewhere," said Arlen. "I couldn't place him at first. And then—" He laughed. "It's nonsense, I expect, but—well, look at *me*."

He sat there, without smiling now, in the pose which Latimer had shown in the photograph which had been widely circulated. Roger stared. Sloan came round to the other side of Arlen's chair, and looked down at him. There was silence in the office, broken by the rumble of trams and the hum of traffic on the Embankment.

"Well?" Arlen asked abruptly.

"Yes, there is a slight likeness," said Roger, cautiously. "I shouldn't call him your double, but—"

"It's a likeness all right," said Arlen. "I don't mind telling you that when I realized it, it shook me. I happen to have a photograph in my pocket." He took out his wallet, and handed Roger a photograph of himself and a handsome, smiling woman. It was head and shoulders only, and had been taken in a good studio. "See what I mean?"

Roger put one of Latimer's photographs by the side of it.

"Well, it's there," said Sloan.

"You can imagine why it shook me," Arlen said. "I didn't discover it until this morning, of course, after I'd decided to come and have a word with you. After that, every time anyone looked at me I thought they were comparing me with this chap. At Paddington, I felt quite sure that a couple of policemen were coming to clap their hands on my shoulders, but they only stared. Your sergeant downstairs positively jumped when he looked up and saw me."

"It isn't such a strong likeness as that," said Roger. "May I borrow this photograph?"

"Er—well, yes. Yes, I suppose so."

"And you've never heard of the man Latimer or, as far as you know, ever seen him before."

"No." Arlen was emphatic.

"Thanks," said Roger, and leaned back and rubbed his eyes. "Did either of your murdered cousins ever talk of any personal worry or anxiety, Mr. Arlen?"

Arlen grinned.

"Never! We had another thing in common; I forgot to tell you about that. Boastfulness. We didn't often foregather; it must be five years since we all met—we happened to be in London at the same time. You should have been there—hearing fishermen telling their stories was nothing to it. Each of us had to beat the other on income, sales record, wife, house—it would have been nauseating if I hadn't seen the funny side of it. Odd thing," went on Arlen, "I knew that I was as bad as the rest, but I think I was the only one who kind of stood outside myself and saw what was happening. They were deadly earnest about it all."

"No reason, as far as you know, why any of them should have been frightened?"

"Good lord, no!"

"Did you ever do business together?"

"No—no cause to."

Roger said: "I've had six names altogether; Mr. Arlen—yours, the two Bennetts in Birmingham and Mrs. Drew, of York, their sister, isn't she? And the two dead men, of course. Have you any other relatives?"

Arlen hesitated again.

"Most people can claim more than five," murmured Roger.

"Well, we were a small family," Arlen said. "And we had rough luck during the wars—some of the family were wiped out, in bombing raids in both of them. And I lost a brother at Arnhem. We six are the only relations who really rate, I think."

"But there's someone else?"

"Er—yes, I suppose so." Arlen wrinkled his nose. "It's a mucky business, this kind of inquiry. All the dirty linen comes out for washing. There *is* another relative, or rather there was. One of my father's brothers, Simon, was a kind of family skeleton. I knew him when I was a child, but he vanished soon afterward. I didn't realize until a few years ago that he was put away—in an asylum. You know how families hush up that kind of thing. He was married and there was one child, I believe —I couldn't prove it, but my mother told me there was."

"Boy or girl?"

"Oh, a male of the species."

"What was his name?"

"Arnold."

"What happened to him?"

Arlen frowned, and looked ill at ease.

"I don't exactly know, but I gathered that it wasn't anything my mother was particularly proud of. The wife died, not long after the child was born, and the kid was farmed out. She told me that she tried to keep in touch with the foster parents, but my—my father and the rest of the family wouldn't have any of it. Not a pretty story, is it?— they could be hard on kids, in the old days. I don't see how it can help, and yet—"

Roger said: "It can help a lot, and you know it, Mr. Arlen. Have you told us everything?"

"All the way up I've been racking my brains to recall everything I can," said Arlen. "My mother was ill when she told me; she died soon afterward. I think she had an attack of conscience and wanted to die with it off her mind. She rambled a bit, but the general outline is about right—my uncle went off the rails and he was homicidal, so they jugged him. Rather than let anyone think there was a taint in the family, it was hushed up. The sickening thing is that they wished the boy onto foster parents, presumably without saying anything about the family history. Ugly kind of business."

"Have you ever discussed this with your cousins?"

"Er—I did once, with Lionel."

"Why Lionel?"

"He was the eldest, and most likely to know something about it. I had a fancy to try to trace the boy, but there wasn't a thing I could do."

"You didn't talk about it to any of the others?"

"No. Wilfred wasn't the type to have any sentiment about a thing like that, I don't know the other Bennetts really well, and their sister—" He shrugged. "She's always been pretty highly strung. Neurotic type. Between you and me she leads her husband a hell of a life. I certainly wouldn't discuss it with her, at any time. I doubt if the other Bennetts know much, although they probably knew a little. I wish I could offer more help, but—well, I thought you'd better know about this. Especially as the man Latimer could be mistaken for me. I mean he *could* be one of the family, couldn't he?"

"Yes. How long are you going to stay in London?"

"Oh, I shall go back tonight. I shan't leave my wife at home alone until you've caught this chap; she'll be too jumpy. Shouldn't be going away, anyhow. I wouldn't have gone this time—to North Wales, I mean—but there was a sticky customer, and I didn't want to lose any business."

"Naturally you didn't," said Roger, and stood up. "You've been very good. We won't worry your wife if it's avoidable, and I think we'll get all we want from some other source. You'll be careful when on the road or on your own, won't you?"

Arlen laughed.

"I tell you, I'll hit first at any suspicious stranger. Don't worry about me—the others were pretty soft, physically." He laughed again, but there was no ring of confidence in it. "Er—I suppose it *could* simply be coincidence."

"Oh, yes. Obviously."

"Not good, feeling that you're next on the list," said Arlen. "I'm thinking of my other cousins, of course; *I'm* all right."

They shook hands; and Sloan saw Arlen downstairs.

"Superintendent Kennedy of Newbury for you, sir," said the operator to Roger.

"Thanks...Hallo, Ken."

"Hallo, Handsome, now what?"

"This man Raymond Arlen," said Roger. "He tells me he reached home soon after seven o'clock last night. Check if you can, will you?"

"Think he was lying?" asked the Newbury Superintendent.

"Just being sure," said Roger.

He drove, with Peel, to Birmingham after an early lunch and reached the home of Ernest Bennett, Merryfield, High Lane, Erdington, a little after half-past three. He had not warned the Bennett brothers that he would be there, and expected first to find Ernest's wife. A modern car was drawn up in the drive of a large house, which was built on the slope of a hill and stood in a large, attractive garden. There was a slight wind, waving the daffodils, some early tulips and wallflowers. A gardener was trimming the edge of a diamond-shaped lawn, and looked at the new arrivals with slow interest.

111

There was a front loggia, and in the room beyond it, reached by French windows, Roger saw the heads of two men, sitting at the far end of the room. Neither of them troubled to look around. The heads were almost identical; the men were gray-haired, each had a bald patch, and their ears stuck out.

A maid answered the door.

There were the usual preliminaries, and then she led Roger and Peel into the room. It was long, and ran right through the house, with French windows at either end. The ceiling was low, there was no picture rail; everything was fresh and clean. The furniture was modern and restrained, the coloring was pastel shades of green and yellow.

Two men, almost identical in height, shape and size, but very different in face, now stood in front of the fireplace, where an electric fire glowed.

The first man held out his hand. He was broad-faced, with a broad nose, a pendulous lower lip and short upper lip. His cheeks were florid, as if he were out of doors a great deal, and he wore horn-rimmed glasses.

"*I* am Ernest Bennett," he said. "Good afternoon, Chief Inspector. This is an unexpected visit. I expected a call from the local police, of course, but not from Scotland Yard. This is my brother, Arthur Bennett."

Arthur had a thin face, sunken cheeks and, when he opened his lips to greet them, showed his gums.

Both men were dressed in striped gray trousers and black coats; both looked prosperous business-men, who might have been found in any city.

"Mosht shurprished," said Arthur Bennett.

Ernest coughed.

"My brother has been to the dentist this morn-

112

ing; you will allow me to do most of the talking, I hope. It's a dreadful affair, dreadful, and we both —*both* greatly appreciate your warning. Not that we can feel it is necessary, but it is as well to be on our guard—yes. Arthur fully agrees with me. However, it has had one distressing result, Chief Inspector."

"I'm sorry about that."

"Our sister—Mrs. Drew. She was on the telephone; *very* upset. Most upset," said Ernest. "She is highly strung and nervous at the best of times, and naturally this has greatly worried her. However, you were doubtless doing only your duty as you conceived it."

"Thanks," said Roger. "This is Detective Sergeant Peel."

Two gray heads nodded, but Ernest had little time for a mere detective sergeant.

"You understand, Chief Inspector, that we are by no means convinced that there is any need for us to feel that we are—er—menaced. Menaced is the word, of course. The deaths of Lionel and Wilfred, deeply regrettable though they are, *could* be unconnected, couldn't they?"

"Of course," said Roger.

"Told you sho," interpolated Arthur, from behind his left hand.

"We knew it, of course; it was obvious," said Ernest, but he couldn't hide his relief. He had really been worried, and that meant he probably felt that he had some cause to worry. "This unhappy affair can be exaggerated, and the family connection is—well, very far-fetched. Very. It would mean that someone had reason to hate us, wouldn't it, Chief Inspector?"

"And no one has?"

"Ridiculous to suggest it!"

"Abshurd," lisped Arthur.

"All of us are good citizens. I like to think that we have played a proper part in the communal and social life of our times. In fact, I know that Arthur and I have; we have made it an unvarying rule. And no one has *any* reason to dislike us. None at all."

"Good," said Roger.

"Shigarette?" asked Arthur, sputteringly explosive.

"Oh, yes, and do sit down," said Ernest, gustily hospitable. "I will arrange for some tea; you must be tired after your long drive. I will—"

He stepped toward the fireplace and a bell push.

"You're very kind," said Roger. "I believe that your uncle, Simon Arlen, had a serious illness many years ago."

Ernest's hand stopped a few inches off the bell push, but his arm didn't drop. Arthur forgot his naked gums, and stared open-mouthed. The words had come out so casually and pleasantly, yet affected them like a physical blow.

Slowly, Ernest lowered his arm.

"Really," said Arthur, weakly.

"So you know about Uncle Simon," said Ernest slowly. "Well, well. Of course—it has nothing to do with this, nothing at all. *Nothing!* It's ridiculous."

"*Abshurd.*"

"It was most unfortunate, but these things happen in any family," said Ernest. "My uncle Simon was injured in the First World War; it deranged him; he was always rather strange—in fact I know that he was advised not to marry, but—well, he was headstrong. Most headstrong. Then he imagined his wife was faithless, and attacked her; that

114

was just before the child was born. A great trag-edy—great tragedy. Of course, we—we were anx-ious to do all we could for the child, and we felt it better that he should not know the—er—the cir-cumstances of being orphaned. We had the respon-sibility, because his brothers—Wilfred's father and Raymond's father, you understand—were dead. Wilfred and Raymond were too young to act. So we—mind you, we were guided by Lionel: Lionel was the eldest—we decided that the best thing to do was to have the child adopted."

He stopped, and moistened his lips; and both men dabbed their foreheads with handkerchiefs.

"How did you know?" asked Ernest.

Roger said casually: "We don't have much diffi-culty getting information, Mr. Bennett. How long ago did this happen?"

"Eh? Well, so long—"

"Shirty-one years," Arthur declared. "Remember it well. Wash twenty-seven myshelf at the time. You'd be shirty, Ernest."

"So the child would be thirty-one," said Roger.

"Sh'right."

"What was his name?"

"Arnold."

"What was the name of the family which adopted him?"

The brothers paused.

Peel coughed suddenly, and made them glance at him sharply. Afterward, there was silence.

"Surely you remember the name," said Roger.

"Well—no." Ernest moistened his lips again. "We agreed with Lionel on the general course of action, but he was the eldest; he handled the whole affair. He preferred to tell us nothing; we—"

Roger said abruptly: "You just wanted to get rid of the child, so that you need never be worried."

"Really!" Ernest raised a hand.

"Sh'right," Arthur said. He stood up and walked restlessly about the room. "It ish right, Ernest. Let'sh faish it. Often shought about it; wicked shing to do." He stood in front of Roger. "You sheriously think his boy might have killed my brother and coushin? Sheriously?"

"Nonsense!" cried Ernest.

Roger said: "It's too early to form any opinion, gentlemen. We're just getting information together. Are you sure that neither of you knows the name of the family which adopted the child?"

Arthur said miserably: "No idea."

"There was no need for us to know," said Ernest sharply. "I am not at all sure that the information is relevant, Chief Inspector."

"Did you ever discuss this with your brother Lionel?"

"Seldom."

"How often?" Roger barked.

"Perhaps once every two or three years. Chief Inspector, I don't like your manner. There is nothing at all reprehensible, and in any case this affair happened many years ago. Occasionally my Uncle Simon's name cropped up in conversations; we would mention it then, in passing."

"You've never tried to trace the child?"

"Certainly not! And Lionel—"

"I did," said Arthur, thickly.

13

York

Ernest gasped: "Arthur!" and backed away from his brother as if in horror.

Arthur looked at him defiantly, but there was something pathetic in his expression when he turned to Roger. He licked his lips and showed his gums again, and completely forgot to hide his mouth behind his hand.

"Yesh, I did. Wanted to get the name from Lionel. He wouldn't tell me—said he'd forgotten —pooh-poohed the whole affair. Sho I went to shee the doctor and nursh. Couple who attended the birth, undershtand. Must be ten years ago now. They couldn't help. Knew the boy had been adopted; Lionel had told them. No laws about it in those days—if there were, Lionel didn't worry about that. I asked at the Town Hall and the Registry Office—no trace of the adoption anywhere. Birsh shertificate was there, of course—thash all."

"Where were you living?" asked Roger.

"London—St. John's Wood," said Ernest, as if he resented being left out of the conversation. "Arthur, I am astonished! If you'd told me, I—well, it was a foolish gush of sentiment. Nothing more or nothing less."

Roger said: "Can you give me the name of the doctor and the nurse, Mr. Bennett?"

"Shink sho," said Arthur, and began to mumble to himself, then took an envelope from his pocket and scribbled notes on it. "There y'are."

"Thanks." Roger put the envelope into his wallet. "Have you read today's newspapers, gentlemen?"

"Coursh," said Arthur.

"Naturally," said Ernest.

"So you've seen the picture of this man."

Roger took out Latimer's photograph.

"I have never seen him before," said Ernest thinly, "and I flatly refuse to believe that there is any connection between these dastardly crimes and the unhappy family affair upon which you have intruded. I must say that I think the police would be better employed if they—"

"Funny shing," said Arthur, cutting across his brother's words, "but I did wonder. Take another look, Ernest. This is a better picsher than the one in the paper."

He took the photograph and thrust it in front of his brother's eyes.

Ernest moved back, then held it at arm's length.

"I have never—" he began, but broke off with a gulp. He shot a startled glance at his brother, looked anywhere but at Roger, and finally took the picture very close to his eyes. "It *can't* be," he said in a strangled voice. "But there *is* a resemblance."

"Raymond. Coushin Raymond," Arthur declared. "Image of him, when he was young. Image. Talk about a family likenesh. No doubt about it at all."

*   *   *

Roger telephoned Sloan from the house, giving the names of the doctor and nurse who had attended Mrs. Simon Arlen.

"Find them tonight," he said.

He drove out of the gates of the house, and sent the car hurtling along the winding road toward Birmingham. Peel sat silent and smoking by his side, knowing his man well, and realizing that this wasn't a moment to speak. Roger turned onto the main road, and the speedometer needle crept up toward the seventy mark; they passed everything on the road. On the approaches to Birmingham, Roger slowed down, took a road signposted Leicester and said: "Look up the road to York in that A.A. book, will you?"

"York?"

"I want to see that sister," Roger said, "and I'd like to get there before it's dark."

Peel flipped over the pages, stopped, and said after a moment: "You're all right for a bit; I'll fix the route in a few minutes. Going to tell anyone?"

"I'll stop a patrol car or a man on the beat and send word," said Roger. "Haven't any appointment tonight, have you?"

He grinned, unexpectedly.

Peel laughed.

"Nothing firm!"

"Seeing Georgina again?"

Peel said: "I know what you were getting at yesterday, but you were jumping to conclusions. As a matter of fact, I thought it might be a good idea to get to know her better. I think she's all right, but I'm not so sure about her sister—Meg's soft on

Latimer. And—er—oh, all right," he added, flushing, "I wouldn't object to getting to know Gina Sharp after hours."

Roger said: "Go easy, until this show is over. You don't want to run yourself into trouble."

Peel said ruefully: "You're making pretty sure I do go easily, aren't you? That's why you've brought me up here."

Roger glanced at him; and Peel was still flushed.

"Listen, Jim," Roger said. "That's pretty clear proof that you're not thinking straight. You know damned well I wouldn't take you with me if I didn't think you were the best man to have. You may or may not get the flutters over Georgina Sharp, but I'm not wet-nursing you."

"Sorry," muttered Peel.

"She was at that flat, and put up a pretty good show. She might have told the simple truth, but she might have been fooling us. There's one thing you've overlooked, Jim."

"What's that?"

"We know—or think we know—that Meg Sharp was in love with Latimer. We don't know whether Gina Sharp had anything else against him. I'm not a bit sure that she would storm his place and go for him in the way she went for you, simply because he'd prized some money out of her sister. Oh, she might have done, but we don't take it as gospel."

"What makes you think I've overlooked it?"

Roger laughed. "You'll do. What about that route?"

They had to stop on the outskirts of York, which they reached as daylight was fading, to get directions to the home of Mrs. Drew. The policeman who directed them finished and said mildly: "Coming along pretty fast, weren't you? Take it easy in this light, sir, please."

Roger smiled. "Thanks, but I'm in a hurry. Will you call your headquarters and tell them that I'm in the district and will turn up sometime this evening?" He handed the man a card, and drove off as a startled face turned toward him. He saw the man grin.

Mrs. Drew lived in a house called Corby, in Willow Lane. There was a small stream, two miles on the eastern side of York, and over it ran a humpbacked bridge with white wooden rails. On one bank willows drooped leafy branches toward the rippling water. In the half light the scene was pleasing, with low, wooded hills and a few houses showing against the skyline. Several narrow roads turned off this, but the constable had been clear: they must go to the end of the road running alongside the stream, and Corby, the house, would be on the right-hand side.

The house loomed out of the dusk as Roger switched on his headlamps. A boy was cycling along near the river, two girls swinging tennis racquets stood at the gate of another house, chatting. Corby, which lay low, had a large garden with the stream running at the end of it. It was a two-story brick house with pebble-dash at the top of the walls, nicely proportioned and, like all the houses in this family, owned by someone in a fairly high income group.

The gates were closed.

Peel glanced at his watch.

"Pretty good time, and you've made it just before dark. Bit eerie, isn't it?"

"Eerie?"

"You know what I mean," said Peel. "That devil could be having another crack."

"At whom?"

"*He* doesn't know you've warned the others," said Peel.

Roger didn't answer, and Peel climbed out to open the gates. As he was bending to pull up the bolt, Roger looked at the house and saw a shadowy figure appear at the side. The figure, of a man, had come from some bushes on the right of the garden. Without looking toward the gate, the man went straight to a window and disappeared.

Roger said sharply: "Peel."

Peel looked up, as he swung open the gate.

"Hurry," said Roger.

He climbed out; starting the engine again would ony warn the man. Was it possible that he'd timed it perfectly, run into another attack? The notion seemed absurd, but he jumped off the drive onto the grass verge, with Peel by his side, and began to run.

"What?" asked Peel, sharply.

"Man at the window," Roger grunted.

There was a light on in one of the front rooms of the house. A woman was outlined against it, with her back to them. She turned, suddenly, as if to pull the curtains—and saw them.

The window was open.

She screamed, splitting the quiet.

Peel gasped: "We'd better slow down, or—"

He broke off as another figure appeared at the window. A man. A hand stretched out and gripped the woman, swinging her round. She screamed again. Roger slid his hand into his pocket, and then shouted: *"Thief!"*

He gasped as he finished, drew out a police whistle and managed to give a long blast, without slowing down. Peel was gaining on him.

The light went out.

They could see nothing in the house now, and could hear only the thud of their own footsteps on the grass. Then Peel kicked into a stone, and went flying. Roger heard his cry and the thud which followed. He didn't stop, but blew the whistle again. The front door of the house was closed, and he veered round toward the side, where the man had appeared. As he neared it, he saw that there were French windows, wide open.

He blew again.

The shrill blast was almost deafening, but it didn't cover the roar of a shot.

Roger reached the corner of the house, and intuitively slackened his pace. He couldn't hear Peel. The echo of the shot still rang in his ears. He reached the loggia, and as he neared the French window a man appeared. He could only see the outline, for it was nearly dark. He didn't see the gun in the man's hand, but flung himself to one side. He thudded against the wall as he saw the flash and heard the roar, lost his footing, and fell. He felt a spasm of terror; fear of death at its worst. He heard another roar, and something hit the wall just above his head. He heard nothing else—no footsteps; nothing. He didn't know how long it took him to get to his feet.

Peel was shouting: *"You there, Roger? You there?"*

Roger called unsteadily: "This way!"

There was a light in a house about a hundred yards away, and a figure appeared against it, running fast. Roger started to run, but his legs wobbled. Peel caught up to him, shouted: "There he is!" and raced past. He didn't see the man again, but went on running. Lights sprang up at other houses; he saw a man come out of a doorway.

There was a shout, farther away but loud and distinct.

Then a car engine started up.

It roared, blasting through the quiet night. Roger couldn't see the car, but heard it moving off. Then it appeared against the light-colored surface of the road, moving away from them. It swung round the corner of a house and disappeared.

Peel was shouting.

Another car started up, and headlights silvered the open doors of a garage. He saw Peel running toward the other car.

Roger slowed down; Peel couldn't be seriously hurt.

Roger heard voices as the car was backed out of the garage; Peel's dark figure appeared by its side, then disappeared into it.

The second car scorched along the road and swung round the corner, but the glow of its headlights showed above the trees and the houses.

Then, from behind him, a woman screamed.

14

Fourth Victim?

Roger's left shoulder and knee were painful; he limped as he hurried toward the house. The light had come on, and the woman screamed again. He broke into a run as the third scream came, but couldn't keep it up. He tripped against the step of the loggia, and nearly fell, biting his lips at the sudden pain. He steadied, and stepped into the room.

A young girl stood in an open doorway, a hand at her mouth, eyes wide in terror.

A woman lay on the floor in the middle of the room, and there was blood on the carpet and on her gray hair.

The girl screamed again: "No, no, no!"

Roger said: "Steady, now. He had to quiet her, had to ignore his wrenched knee. He reached the woman and knelt down. "Telephone for a doctor— quickly, please."

"What is it?" a man called. "What is it?"

"Get the doctor!" Roger rasped.

The girl turned and ran out of the room.

The woman was unconscious, and might be

dead. The blood came from a wound in her fore-head; she was lying on her side, and the wound was uppermost. Her legs were bent, and she lay awkwardly with an arm doubled up beneath her. He felt her pulse; she was alive.

He moved the gray hair aside, gently. There was some bleeding. He straightened up, and a man said: "This is—dreadful."

He was tall, gray, distinguished-looking—and there was horror in his eyes.

"Lily," he said, and came forward.

Roger said: "She is alive. Is that doctor on the way?"

"My—my daughter's calling him. This is—*terrible*."

"It could be worse. Get blankets and hot-water bottles, quickly, and have some tea made—very sweet."

He hurried out with the man, and they reached the kitchen. Roger took a bowl of water and a towel.

"Where's your antiseptic kept?"

"Eh? Oh, there's a bottle here."

The man was putting on a kettle.

"I'll bathe the wound," Roger said.

The bleeding wasn't serious, and he had finished when the man came back with blankets and a hot-water bottle.

"Where were you when it happened?" Roger asked.

"In the garden shed. I thought I heard a shot and couldn't understand it; then I heard a second. I hurried round—the shed's at the bottom of the garden." The man still looked dazed. "There was nothing else I could do; some men were running, there were cars. This is—*terrible*."

126

The girl came along the passage outside.

Roger said again: "She's alive, and with luck we shall have her in the hospital in no time."

He went across to a telephone in the corner, lifted the receiver and asked for the police. The man stared at him, the girl at the woman.

"Police Station, can I help you?"

"This is Inspector West of Scotland Yard. I want an ambulance at a house named Corby, in Willow Lane, as quickly as you can get it here. Then give me the C.I.D."

"Yes, sir!"

It was only a second before another man with a deep Yorkshire voice spoke.

"Chief Inspector *West?*"

"Yes, Latimer's been here." Roger couldn't be sure of that; it might not have been Latimer, but the name would work like a charm. "He's driven off from Willow Lane, pursued by my sergeant in a commandeered car. Have the net spread fast and as wide as you can make it—warn all other stations, and—"

"We'll get him!"

"He's still armed."

"We'll fix *him* all right," the man said, and then broke off. "But—"

"Yes?"

"Did you say Willow Lane?"

"Yes."

"But we've had a man there all day, just to make sure that it couldn't happen."

Roger said: "You'd better get some men up here as soon as you can; they might find your chap."

He rang off, and wiped his forehead. Now both the man and the girl were looking at the woman. Husband and daughter, he thought. His knee was aching, but he could walk, and there was hardly any trouble at his shoulder.

The girl began to cry.

The man said: "This is—terrible."

An unconscious policeman was found near the shed at the end of the garden; he was not seriously hurt.

The Drew's doctor, a middle-aged and noncommittal man, went with Mrs. Drew to the hospital. Neighbors were thronging the house. Then a brisk young Detective Inspector took control, arranged for Drew to go into York to wait at the hospital, and for the daughter, whose name was Victoria, to stay with neighbors. She left the house in a daze.

The police surgeon examined Roger's knee, diagnosed a slight sprain and bound it securely.

"Don't try it too much, and you'll be all right," he said. "Painful?"

"A bit."

"Take three aspirins and a noggin."

The brisk Detective Inspector came across to them. Roger was sitting back in an easy chair, near the telephone. Outside it was quite dark; there was concealed lighting in the room. The Detective Inspector had a broad face, an amiable smile and a broad dialect.

"I'm glad to meet one of the big men of the Yard," he said, with a boyish grin. "Don't get much nearer you people than the newspapers, mostly. What brought you up here just now? I've heard you're supposed to have a bloodhound's nose; but it was more than that, wasn't it?"

"I wanted to see Mrs. Drew, and thought it as good a time as any," Roger said. He didn't try to explain the urge which had driven him so fast along the road; few would believe him. "Well, now we're pretty sure about the lie of the land—it's a family vendetta."

"You try telling my superintendent that," said the Detective Inspector.

Roger grinned. "You try! While we're here I'd like to go through all Mrs. Drew's papers, and her husband's, for that matter, looking for anything about a boy child born to her mother's brother Simon, thirty-one years ago. How many men can you put onto the job?"

"We can be through in a couple of hours," said the Yorkshireman.

There were no helpful documents; nothing to suggest that Mrs. Drew knew anything about Latimer. No connection with the rest of the case was found, except that she was one of the small family of blood relations of the late Simon Arlen.

From his room at the Black Swan Hotel, Roger called Janet; Sloan had already told her that he wouldn't be back that night, and she was cheerful enough. Then he called Sloan, who was still at the Yard.

"Hallo, Roger. Get him?"

"No. Peel came back half an hour ago—they lost the devil. I don't know how he's managed it, but he's slipped through. Keep everyone closely watched; he may sneak back to London, and one of them has probably been lying. Any word from the Sharp women, at Middleton Street?"

"No, nothing."

"From Newbury?"

"There is a bit," said Sloan.

"Raymond Arlen?"

"Believe it or not, he lied about the time he

reached home last night. It was after nine. His wife said half past seven, but a neighbor saw him drive in at five past nine. He had time to get from St. Albans, if he had a car nearby and stepped on it."

"Well, well! And he was away from home the night of the first murder."

"That's right."

"Have you checked him in North Wales?"

"Not yet—give me a chance. But he didn't go home to Newbury today, Roger. He wasn't there half an hour ago, when I telephoned."

"Well, *well!*" breathed Roger. "Put out a call for Mr. Raymond Arlen."

"It's out," said Sloan. "Not for the press yet, though."

"No, not yet." Roger hesitated. "About Latimer, now. Have you dug up anything more about his past?"

"Nothing." Yet Sloan was obviously excited. "I've been wondering if Raymond Arlen could have a double identity. He's away from home a lot, and might have run the flat at Mayfair. Tell me I'm letting my imagination run away with me, if you like, but it's odd."

"Any luck with that doctor and nurse?"

"Not really. We traced them, but the doctor died six months ago; the nurse simply attended the confinement," said Sloan. "I—half a minute, the other telephone's buzzing."

Roger looked at the cream-colored wallpaper of the large bedroom with twin beds—he was to share it with Peel, who was still at the local police station. The new development set his mind racing, shook him out of the disappointment at having lost the assailant. Sloan was off the wire for a long time, and footsteps sounded at the door. Peel came in, whistling.

Sloan said tensely: "You there?"

"Yes."

"Margaret Sharp's missing," said Sloan. "Georgina's just reported it. She went out early afternoon, didn't keep a teatime appointment, and hasn't come back."

"Find her!" said Roger.

He and Peel were ready for the road at half past seven next morning.

The only news was that Mrs. Drew would recover.

Roger limped into his office a little after two o'clock, after the long drive shared with Peel at the wheel. Sloan, in his shirt sleeves and with his tie hanging loose, was speaking into the telephone; he sounded short-tempered. He banged the receiver down, and glared up at Roger, realized who it was, and forced a grin.

"Trouble?" asked Roger.

"Everything's trouble. Raymond Arlen hasn't turned up, Meg Sharp is still missing, and we've had about seven hundred more reports of Latimer. Seen the papers?"

"No."

"The only one that's behaving itself is the *Echo*," said Sloan disgustedly. "The others are giving us a towsing for letting Latimer go. The Yorkshire police have got it in the neck, too; but you're blamed —you were on the spot, weren't you? The *Echo* runs the story that you saved her life; the others give a grudging admission. It's merry hell. Chatworth is like a bear with a sore head, and keeps yelling for you. Better go and see him," added Sloan; "you're about the only one who can calm him down."

The door opened.

"Oh, *is* he?" growled the Assistant Commissioner, and thrust the door back with a bang. He slammed it, and came toward them aggressively. "Where have you been, West?"

"York," said Roger promptly.

"You didn't have to stay there all night."

"Sorry," said Roger, briefly.

"You're no more than a log of wood. I can't understand what's got into you. Don't you realize there have been three murders and one near murder, and three people are running around loose, cocking a snook at us? If there's one thing I won't have, it's being made to look ridiculous."

Roger didn't speak.

Chatworth growled. "I can understand Latimer. I can just understand Raymond Arlen. But I thought we were supposed to be watching this Margaret Sharp."

Roger said: "There's nothing easier than shaking off a man, if you want to do it; we can't blame anyone for that."

"Who was watching her?"

"I don't know, I—"

"You don't *know.*"

"It was Detective Officer Smithson, sir," said Sloan, daringly. "Mr. West wasn't—"

"See Smithson, find out why he's sleeping on his job," said Chatworth, and ran his hand over his bald patch. "Pick up those missing people. And make sure there aren't any more Arlen relatives in the London area. Warn Birmingham; they'll be fools if they let anything happen to the Bennetts."

132

He stormed out.

Sloan gasped: "Phew! What's got into him?"

"Just sent to try us," said Roger. "He's not looking so good, did you notice?"

"Trust you to make an excuse. But when you come to think of it, it's damned bad. Three people we can't lay our hands on. If anything happens to them—" Sloan broke off, and laughed. "No sense in losing my head, but I've had a hell of a day." The telephone bell rang. "That damned thing just won't stop ringing; there isn't a minute left to breathe." He snatched off the receiver. "Sloan!" he barked.

He listened, scowling; the scowl faded into blackness and then tension.

He said: "Sure?"

He listened....

He put down the receiver slowly.

"Raymond Arlen's dead," he said. "Killed—shot—a few miles from his home. He's been dead some hours."

Mrs. Raymond Arlen, her face composed, sat awkwardly in a large chair at her home. The astonishing thing about the homes of this family was their similarity; they seemed to have been made on the same pattern; had excellent sites, the same charm of decor, the same delicate coloring.

The woman was in her late thirties, and sat with hands on the arms of her chair. She wore a flowered smock, to disguise her figure. She looked plump and well; the shock hadn't made her lose her color. She'd been told of the murder by a local doctor, some time before Roger had arrived at the house on the outskirts of Newbury.

"I'm sorry; I know I shouldn't, but I lied about it.

Raymond asked me to say he was in just after seven; I don't know why he should. So when I was asked, that's what I said. As a matter of fact, I was longing for him to come home. It's a big house, and the servants were at the back, and I get so nervous these days."

"Don't you know why he asked you to say that?"

"I just haven't any idea, I assure you." She closed her eyes. "Then he left home yesterday morning, and said that he would be back by tea time. When he didn't get back, I was worried, but I didn't want to call the police. I did, in the end. It began to prey on my mind, because—"

She stopped, and tears flooded her eyes.

Roger didn't prompt her.

"Because someone had rung me up and said he was very like the photograph of this man Latimer. Oh, I know it was silly, it was disloyal; but once an idea like that gets into your head—it would have been different if he'd been at home, but he wasn't. And then I heard about the attack on Lily, over the ten o'clock news. I was—frantic! And then—this. This!" She closed her eyes, and tears spilled onto her cheeks, her voice was husky, but she went on speaking. "Mr. West, please—please tell me, did he kill himself? Did he?"

Roger said: "He was shot at close quarters, Mrs. Arlen, in exactly the same way as the others, except that he wasn't in a car. He obviously met his murderer by appointment. And it must have been someone he knew. We're anxious to find out who it might have been—and that means we want a list of his friends, and especially anyone he's seen largely."

She didn't answer.

"Has he been worried recently?"

"No, I don't think so. He was always cheerful. I shall miss him—so much. It's hard to believe that he's dead. Mr. West, you're not lying to me, are you? He didn't—*kill* the others and then—then shoot himself?"

"He did not, Mrs. Arlen. Have you ever heard him mention the name Latimer?"

"No."

"Has he been away lately, without any apparent reason?"

"He travels about so much," said Mrs. Arlen. "As a matter of fact, I—I've wondered. I couldn't help it, but I've wondered if he were keeping something back from me. He knows I'm very jumpy when I'm like this, and I've known him to keep back bad news. For the last few weeks he—he *has* seemed more thoughtful than usual. Withdrawn. But I haven't the slightest idea why."

Roger learned nothing more from her.

But when he went to the Newbury Police Station, there was a report from Scrymegour of the Yard. The bullets which had been fired at Mrs. Drew and had killed Raymond Arlen had come from the same gun; the gun that had killed the other three men.

Georgina Sharp said: "But how can I help being worried? Don't be so silly!"

"Sorry," said Peel.

"She's been missing for nearly twenty-four hours now," said Georgina, who was sitting in her flat, legs beneath her, arm resting on the arm of the settee. The pose was sheer beauty. "I can't understand it, but it's not any use saying it isn't like her. She's always been unpredictable. I think she's gone to Latimer; he's got a wicked hold over her. I sensed it before; that's why I felt so wild. *Can't* you find her?"

Peel was standing in front of her.

"We will," he said.

"You haven't cut much ice yet," Georgina said wearily. "Instead of searching this place, you ought to be looking for her." She drew in her breath. "And if you say 'orders are orders,' I'll scream!"

Peel turned away.

Two detective officers were in the bedroom, going through Meg Sharp's papers. Peel went in to them, and found them sitting on the side of the bed, running through an old deed box.

"Found anything?" asked Peel.

"As a matter of fact," said one of the men, looking up, "I think I have—here." He held up a long slip of paper. "It's an old birth certificate—April, thirty-one years ago, and records the birth of a son, named Arnold, to Simon and Winifred Arlen. What are they doing with *that*?"

15

Relations

Georgina Sharp stood by the window, where her sister had been when Roger had last seen her. Roger, the certificate in his hand, was watching her closely. Peel stood by the door, his face set. The other men had gone, but everything they had found was on a table by Roger's side; there were several other documents, equally significant.

"I tell you I've never heard of that certificate, Arnold and Simon Arlen, or anything about it," Georgina said tautly. "Are you calling me a liar?"

"I'm trying to find out the truth."

"That was Meg's box. She had the key. She had a right to her own private deed box, hadn't she? She was always careful about personal things. I've never seen her open the box; sometimes I've teased her about it. That's *all*."

"Your sister has never talked about the past?"

"No!"

"How long have you been living here together?"

"For eight years, on and off. I was in the WAAF for nearly three; Meg was here; she did a lot of Red Cross work."

"So you came to live with your sister when you were sixteen."

"Yes. I'd lived with Mother until then; when she died Meg made room for me. We've managed to get along smoothly most of the time." Georgina's eyes were bright with anxiety; perhaps with fear. "She's older than I; she's always had one man or another in tow; that's the only thing we've ever quarreled about. She made herself cheap, but—oh, what does *that* matter?"

Roger said: "You are full sisters, aren't you?"

"Yes!"

"I've reason to doubt that," said Roger formally, and picked up another paper. "This is another birth certificate, Miss Sharp—your sister's. She was the child of Charles and Millicent Latimer. Here's another." He picked up the third, while Georgina stared at him, hands clenched at her sides, expression hostile and frightened. "This is yours—you were born to Alfred and Millicent Sharp. And there's a marriage certificate; that of Alfred Sharp and Millicent Latimer, the widow of Charles Latimer. You and Meg are half-sisters. Do you mean to tell me that you didn't know it?"

"I did not!"

"Can you think of any reason why your sister should keep the truth from you?"

"No!" cried Georgina. "It isn't true; it can't be true!"

"Why did you lose your temper when you thought Detective Sergeant Peel was Latimer? Why attack him so viciously?"

"I've told you."

"You say your sister has always been brazen with her men friends, yet you weren't resigned to

138

it, were so furious that you completely lost your self-control. Why? What's the truth?"

"I've told you the truth. He had some influence over her, stronger than any of the others. She'd never let a man rob her before. He could do anything he liked with her; she was hopelessly in love—"

"*Was* she?" asked Roger, softly. "Although they were so closely related."

"It's all very well for you to talk now you've discovered this," Georgina stormed at him. "I knew he could twist her round his little finger; I thought she'd really fallen in love with him. Instead—"

"What?"

"Isn't it obvious? He had some other hold on her. It must have been—blackmail."

Roger said more easily: "You've always suspected that he was using a kind of blackmail, haven't you? That's what made you so angry, why you went to see him?"

She didn't answer.

"Isn't it?"

"I didn't *know*," Georgina said defiantly. "I just couldn't understand why she was behaving like that. I wanted to find out the truth. It was a funny business altogether. I—I haven't told you everything," she went on, and pressed her hand against her burning forehead. "It didn't seem to matter, I don't think it does matter. It wasn't that Meg couldn't hold her man—she turned them down, one after the other. I could never understand it, but that's what happened. With Latimer it was different. It's hard to say how, but he seemed to matter to her much more than the others. It just wasn't the same kind of attraction. I sensed that, and wanted to find out what was behind it. Now—

you mean that they were brother and sister." Her voice was husky.

"Relations, anyhow," said Roger.

"Couldn't—*couldn't* it be a coincidence in the names?"

"Is that likely? Miss Sharp, you know why we're so anxious to find Latimer. You know why we have to make sure that he can't do any more harm. Sure that you know nothing more?"

"Yes," she said wearily. "I'm quite sure."

"You realize that your sister may be in danger, don't you?"

She nodded.

"And if you're holding anything back—"

"I'm not," she said, wearily. "I don't know where she went, I don't know whether they met again. I've told you everything now. If you let him kill Meg—" She caught her breath. "You mustn't allow it."

"We'll find him," said Roger. "But until we do, we want to make sure that nothing can happen to you. I shall leave a man outside this house, back and front. One of them will follow you wherever you go. There's nothing to stop you from evading him, but you'll be asking for trouble if you do."

"Why should I?" she asked flatly.

"If Latimer's holding your sister by force, he may try to do a deal with you—her freedom for more of your money. Don't try anything, don't trust him an inch, for anyone's sake. If you do, and get caught, you'll have walked into it with your eyes wide open. Understand?"

"Oh, I understand," she said.

Roger folded up the certificates and put them in his pocket, nodded, and went to the door. Peel opened it, and looked round at Georgina before he followed Roger out of the flat.

They went downstairs in silence, and stood by Roger's car, looking up and down the street. Detective Officer Smithson was on the other side, but Roger didn't beckon him.

"How bad is it, Jim?" he asked quietly.

"Not so good," said Peel.

"Like to be shifted to another job?"

"It's up to you," said Peel. "I don't think I'll let anything stand in the way of catching Latimer. I think I'd make a better job of following Gina than anyone else—I've two reasons for wanting to keep her out of danger."

Roger looked at him steadily.

"You know what this means? She's one of the family which adopted Simon Arlen's son. She probably knew that, is probably lying. If you fall down on the job, you'll probably get an 'I-can-never-forgive-myself' complex."

"I'll risk it, if you will."

"All right," said Roger. "Watch Georgina. The danger period will be after dark, so take turn and turn with Smithson over there."

Peel said: "Thanks, Roger."

Roger got into the car and drove off, as Peel went across the road to see Smithson. His knee was aching, but not painful; he'd probably used it too much on the drive from York. That didn't slow him down. At the Yard he telephoned Chatworth's office from the hall, and Chatworth was still in.

Roger went straight to his room.

"Now what?" asked Chatworth, gruffly. "Found Margaret Sharp's body?"

"Not yet," said Roger, and dropped the certificates on the desk. "The indications are that she

141

and Latimer had a few secrets between them. She was born Latimer; I think it's pretty certain that Simon Arlen's son was adopted by her family, the Latimers—and that Margaret, who took the name of Sharp, knew it. Her mother married again; Georgina Sharp is a child of the second marriage. It's pretty plain that Margaret knew her foster brother was a dangerous individual, but just how much she knew about his plans is anyone's guess. It's possible that she's gone off to try to stop him from doing anything else."

"What makes you think she thinks she might have any influence over him?" asked Chatworth.

Roger didn't speak.

"All right, follow your hunch if you think it will get you anywhere," said Chatworth. "You didn't lose anything by following the hunch which took you to York last night. Roger, we must get results. I've spent a lot of time with the Home Secretary today. You know the general situation—too much violence, lack of public confidence in the police. A case like this with a man running round killing as he likes is shaking everyone up. I don't like quarreling with the Home Secretary."

"About what, in particular?" asked Roger.

Chatworth growled: "You."

"So that's it." Roger forced a smile. He thought hard before he spoke with great deliberation. "I've had to take plenty of criticism in the past, and it's always worked out all right; but if you'd like to shift me from the job, I shan't argue."

"Want to throw your hand in?"

"No."

Chatworth glowered.

"I've told the Home Secretary that I've more confidence in you than in anyone else here, that

I'm sure you'll get quick results. Get them. If you don't, we'll all be in the cart."

"A general shake-up?" asked Roger, mildly.

Chatworth growled: "I told them that while we're understaffed these crimes of violence are going to get worse, and that if they're not satisfied with what we're doing, they can find someone else to hold down my job. Quick results in this might make them see sense. And don't forget that this is in confidence, young Roger. Off with you!"

Roger went out briskly, reached his office and was glad that Sloan wasn't there. He sat back, lit a cigarette, and frowned at the window.

It was now clear that Chatworth had been under heavy pressure from the Home Office for some time; equally clear that he, West, had come in for sharp criticism. It was characteristic of Chatworth to defend him vigorously with the great Panjandrums, and be ill-tempered and surly to his face. Chatworth was worried because the Yard was under fire; he could foresee an avalanche of criticism coming from the press and public if this case weren't quickly settled.

Roger had no idea where to find Latimer; his only success had been the result of a leap in the dark.

Or the dusk....

It was dusk now. The sun had gone, and the lights were shining over Westminster Bridge and on the Embankment. He stood up, and saw the car lights and the bright windows of the trams clattering alongside the river. This was the hour at which Latimer had struck each night.

Latimer?

Was there any sense in doubting whether Latimer was the man he wanted?

143

*   *   *

Smithson was smarting under his earlier failure, and was prepared to work all hours to make up for it. He was a tall, big, dark-haired man, who had done well at the Yard, and now saw his prospects of promotion being dimmed. He watched Roger drive away, and had the satisfaction of seeing the great man nod to him, affably enough; you could rely on Handsome not to harbor a grievance.

Peel joined him.

"Come to tell me to go home and take a refresher course?" he asked glumly.

"You know Handsome," said Peel. "We're both still on the job. You're due for a spell off duty, but you don't have to take it. We need transport, but not a Yard car—she'd guess what it was. Haven't you a car?"

"I've a two-seated Singer, but—"

"Go and get it, will you?" asked Peel. "Georgina Sharp might try the same trick as her sister, and I don't want to be fooled again. If she goes on foot I can follow and you can keep just behind us, and we'll have transport if she takes a car or a bus. I doubt if she'll move much before dark, if she moves at all. How long will it take you to get your car?"

"Half an hour." Smithson was eager. "I'll make it in twenty minutes, if I can."

"If I'm not about when you get back, call the Yard," said Peel.

"Right!" Smithson hurried off.

Peel strolled along the road, reached the corner and looked back at Number 122. A few people were walking along the street, doors kept opening and closing, but that of 122 kept closed. He smoked a cigarette, and tried to get his own thoughts and emotions in proper order. He could no more explain why Georgina Sharp appealed to him so much than he could explain why he'd never before been particularly interested in women.

It was getting dark; dusk would linger for a long time yet, and he didn't like it. Those grim forebodings which had come at dusk, after the second murder, gathered darkly about him. He told himself that it was nonsense, that nothing would happen tonight; but he wasn't sure.

A car turned into the street, and passed him; it was Smithson in his green two-seater. Smithson pulled up a little farther along the street. More people passed up and down, and Peel kept the door of Number 122 in sight all the time; he was only twenty yards away, and could see the doorway in the poor light of a street lamp.

Suddenly a woman appeared. Peel quickened his pace and approached.

It was Georgina.

16

Meg

Georgina Sharp did not look round, but she knew that Peel was following her. She turned the corner and hurried on toward Kensington High Street. Here the lighting was better. She glanced round from the High Street, and saw Peel only ten yards or so behind her, and she noticed a small car turn the corner, with only its sidelights on. She didn't think anything about the car; it certainly wasn't like a police car.

She crossed the road, so that she was walking along the pavement in the same direction as the traffic. Buses lumbered past, a cyclist tried to pass one on the inside, and brushed close to her. Private cars and taxis made up the stream of traffic. She reached the street opposite the Underground station, and hesitated as if she were about to cross again.

Peel caught up with her.

"Are you crazy?" he asked.

She didn't answer, but swung away and walked on, putting several yards between them. Peel followed doggedly, and Smithson in his two-seater kept coming along, in little bursts. At the corner of High Street and Church Street Georgina hesitated again. Two buses and some taxis were lined up before a traffic light. She hurried round the corner and, as Peel reached it, he saw her put her hand at a taxi. It swerved in to the curb. She peered through the gloom at Peel as she jumped inside, without giving herself time to speak to the driver.

"Quick," she said as she dropped onto the seat. "Straight on."

The driver changed gear and they moved off.

"Go up to Notting Hill Gate and then to Edgware Road," said Georgina. "Near Praed Street."

"Okay, Miss."

The driver was huddled up in many coats, and didn't trouble to look round. Georgina glanced out of the window, and saw no sign of Peel. She caught a glimpse of a small car, one of several, but didn't give it any further thought. Her driver swung up Church Street into Notting Hill and along the Bayswater Road, and then he took side streets which eventually brought him out into the Edgware Road.

Georgina had looked round several times, but hadn't noticed anything to worry about. The small car was hidden by other traffic most of the time. She sat on the edge of her seat, and tapped the glass partition behind the driver. He pushed it farther open, still without looking at his fare.

"Do you know Pullinger Street?"

"Eh?"

"Pullinger Street; it's somewhere off Edgware Road, near Praed Street."

"Sure, I know it," said the driver.

He swung left, made several more abrupt turnings, and eventually slowed down at the end of a long street which looked dim and dismal. There were few lights. He pulled in at the curb, and asked: "What number?"

"This will do."

She paid the driver before getting out. As she stepped from the taxi, a small car passed the end of the street, going very fast; it showed as a green flash beneath a street lamp. No one else was about; of course, it wasn't possible for Peel to have caught up with her. Yet she waited as the taxi drew off, looking up and down, as if afraid of seeing Peel materialize like a wraith. Two people walked hurriedly toward her, one behind the other, and vanished round the corner. Then silence fell, broken only by the tinny sound of music from a radio in one of the houses. She clutched her coat more tightly, and hurried away from the corner, glancing at the numbers on the fanlights of the houses. These opened straight onto the pavement; there were no front gardens and no areas; it was a dismal district. She walked past a big gap in the houses, which made the street look as if it were a gigantic mouth with some teeth extracted, and at the next number—51—she paused. Again she looked up and down the street. A car passed on the other side of the road, but it was too dark for her to recognize it.

She went to Number 53, and banged nervously at the door. The banging sounded very loud. A man slouched past, looking at her curiously, and two boys on bicycles weaved their way along. One of them whistled at her.

No one came to the door.

She knocked again, very loudly; then stepped back and looked at the window which fronted the street. It was in darkness, and she could just make out the curtains inside the room, and the leaves of an aspidistra, one of them brushing against the glass.

She shivered.

She knocked again, and now she was biting her lips in vexation.

The door opened—without any warning—before she heard a sound.

"Oh!" she exclaimed.

The door creaked, and she saw no one beyond, but as she stepped forward, the door closed sharply. It was quite dark.

"Meg!" she gasped; and there was fear in the cry.

A hand closed over her mouth.

She started to scream, and the hand pressed more tightly, another clutched at her throat and pressed. She felt stifled. It lasted only for a moment, but it seemed as if her lungs would burst. She knew the fear of death. Then the hand was taken away, and a man said gruffly: "Don't make a sound."

She stood quivering.

"Where—where's Meg?" she whispered hoarsely.

For answer, the man shifted his hand from her mouth, and held her wrist, twisted her arm behind her, and then pushed her along the narrow passage. She was not aware of anything but the darkness and the tightness of his hold and pain at her elbow. He forced her to turn right, and kicked open a door. A candle burned in a small room beyond, and she saw its reflection in a mirror over the mantelpiece. The man pushed her farther in, then closed the door behind him, with his foot; it was astonishing that he could do it so quietly. He let her go, and she leaned heavily against a round table, which gave a little beneath her weight.

"Quiet," the man repeated.

He wore a hat, pulled low over his eyes, and a scarf drawn up over the lower part of his face. The candlelight gleamed on his eyes, but she couldn't be sure that it was Latimer. As she recovered, she scanned the corners for her sister, but there was no sign of Meg.

"Did you bring the money?"

She mouthed: "Yes."

"Where is it?"

She dipped her hand into the V of her blouse, and drew out a bundle of one-pound notes. He snatched them away.

"How many?"

"Twenty-three," she said. "That's all—"

"It's not enough, I've got to have more!"

"It's all I had! Where's Meg, where—"

"She went out," he said. "She said she was going to get me some food, but she isn't back. Give me your hand." He pulled at her wrist, and the single diamond in the ring on her right hand showed yellow and bright in the gentle light. "I'll have that," he said. "Take it off."

"But—"

"*Give it to me!*" He almost screeched the words.

She took the ring off, and he snatched it. She could hear his labored breathing; he was a man desperately afraid. She still couldn't be sure that it was Latimer, although she felt almost certain it was.

"Were you followed?"

"No!"

"Sure?"

"There was a man in Middleton Street, but I dodged him."

"I hope you did," he said.

"*Where's Meg?*"

"I've told you."

"I don't believe—"

"I've told you!" the man snarled, and gripped her wrist again, twisting it painfully. "Listen. I didn't kill anyone—understand? I didn't kill them; it's a frame-up—I wouldn't kill anyone. But they'll get me for it, if they catch me. I must get out of the country. Meg said she would help me, she promised—"

"*Where is Meg?*"

"You little damned fool, she went out; she hasn't come back. You wait here for her; I daren't wait any longer. Tell her to meet me at the usual place, sometime after midnight. If she lets me down—"

He didn't go on, but twisted Georgina's wrist until she gasped in pain.

"I didn't kill anyone," he muttered.

The words sounded absurd; almost petulant. He let her go, pushed past her, and went into the hall. He closed the door, but she didn't hear the key turn in the lock. She took a step after him, opened the door an inch and saw him disappearing into one of the rooms which led off the passage nearer the front door. She could just make out his shape; he made no sound. Her own courage was returning, and she turned abruptly and went across to the fireplace. There was a long poker, part of an old-fashioned set of fire irons. She picked the poker up and went back to the door—but he burst in before she realized that he was coming. He didn't seem to notice the poker, but gave a strangled cry.

151

"The police!"

He struck at her, and she fell to one side; the poker banged against the wall. He saw it for the first time, bent down and snatched it up. She was sliding down the wall when she saw him rush to a corner of the room, where a window was curtained with some gay folkweave. He pulled this aside, thrust the window up and climbed out. As he did so, there was a thud at the front door.

She got up and went unsteadily toward the passage.

A shout came from the back garden, followed by a thud and a clatter, as if a man had kicked against a dustbin. Thudding came again at the front door. Georgina rushed toward that, aware of the other sounds, terrified without quite knowing why. She opened the door and heard Peel's voice; she couldn't recognize him because he was against the dim light.

"Where is he?"

The dustbin lid clattered again.

Peel pushed past her, and she knocked against the wall. He disappeared into the candlelit room, and she heard him shout: "Smithson!"

There was no answer.

She followed him and stood in the doorway, trembling now. He disappeared through the window, calling the detective's name again. In between his calls there was silence. She thought she heard an exclamation, which was followed by a hush, then by quick footsteps. Peel appeared at the window, his face clear enough in the candlelight. He went past her like the wind, and as he reached the front door, blew a police whistle. It sounded deafening. She stood against the wall, hearing odd sounds—a man running, another whistle, from farther away, and then muttering voices. Then running footsteps followed, and Peel came back. He looked at her without speaking; there was contempt in his eyes. He went out by the window.

She followed him, and there was just sufficient light for her to see him bending down over another huddled figure. Then a policeman in uniform came along the passage, saw her, and said: "Now take it easy, Miss."

His voice was quiet and reassuring; she was glad of his hand on her shoulder. She allowed him to lead her to a chair, as another policeman entered. By then Peel was hoisting Smithson up, with the help of a policeman, and they carried him through the window. Even in that dim light she could see the ugly mark over his forehead and knew that it had been caused by the poker.

A car screamed up outside.

Peel shot another searing glance at Georgina, as he helped to carry Smithson through the room. She didn't know whether the man was badly hurt. She leaned back, with her eyes closed, conscious of the sounds that the others were making. A deep, authoritative voice sounded in the hall, but not that of anyone she knew. Her head ached, her wrist and elbow ached; it wouldn't be easy to forget how Latimer had gripped her wrist.

Peel said: "Let's have some more light."

"The bulb's gone," said a constable.

"Get one from another room."

"Yes, sir."

Georgina knew that Peel was standing alone with her in the room, but he didn't speak. The other sounds seemed to be farther away now, fading voices. They grew stronger, suddenly, and then faded again; she was losing her self-control, and thought she was going to faint. She made herself sit upright, gritting her teeth. She knew that a second man was in the room, but she didn't think about what he was doing until a bright light flashed against her eyes; a bulb was in the socket.

The glare hurt her eyes.

Peel said: "Now try the upstairs rooms, and—"

His voice broke off, and Georgina sensed the reason; he had been shocked into silence. The policeman gave a little gasp, which trailed off.

She opened her eyes.

Meg was lying in a huddled heap in the corner, partly hidden by a chair.

17

Mystery Man?

Georgina screamed: "No!" and sprang out of the chair, past the startled and silent men. She flung herself on her knees beside Meg, and pulled at her hands. Meg's legs were bent under her, her head was propped against the wall; it slipped a little as Georgina pulled. Her cheeks were very pale. Her dress had been torn, and one creamy shoulder showed through. "No!" screamed Georgina. "Meg, wake up; Meg, listen to me; it's Gina! Oh, Meg, Meg!"

A hand touched her shoulder.

"Steady," said Peel.

He helped her up, and she didn't resist. He supported her back to the chair, and now there was only pity, not anger, in his gaze.

"Take it easy," he said, and turned back to Meg.

The policeman was already on one knee beside her, and the shadow of his helmet was long against the wall and over Meg's face. Georgina wanted to close her eyes and shut the scene out, but couldn't. She followed every movement with a fascinated attention—the constable feeling Meg's pulse, Peel bending down and peering into Meg's face. She didn't realize at first that she was holding her breath; then she began to take short, shallow breaths.

"*She's* not dead," said the constable.

"Not—*dead?*"

"I can see that," said Peel, and there was a world of relief in his voice. He turned round to Georgina. "No need to worry." He flashed a smile, and then, with the policeman, began to straighten Meg out. She looked so big, lying at full length.

Georgina jumped up and took a cushion from a chair and carried it across to the others. Now she could see that Meg was breathing, although she still looked dreadfully pale.

"Blankets," said Peel.

"Yes, sir," said a man from the door.

Peel straightened up, and looked at Georgina, and gave a tight-lipped smile. Footsteps sounded on the stairs, heavy and deliberate; but the man was soon back with blankets, which they wrapped round Meg.

"A doctor will be here in a few minutes, sir," said the constable who had brought the blankets. "Soon as I saw her, I sent for one."

"Good."

Peel stood up and joined Georgina, but another car pulled up outside before he spoke. The doctor? She wanted to rush to the door, but Peel put a hand on her shoulder and prevented her from moving.

"Is Sergeant Peel here?"

Georgina recognized West's voice.

"Yes, sir."

"Here," Peel called, and turned away from her.

They met in the doorway, and Peel lowered his

voice, so that Georgina could not hear what he said. The whispered consultation was soon over, and West said in a clearer voice: "Take her into the other room."

She let Peel take her. She walked as if in a daze, and was glad to sit down in a small front parlor. The electric lamp was not so good here, but it showed the photographs on the walls, the tassels of the lampshade, the old-fashioned plush furniture, the oilcloth on the floor. There was little room to move, because there was so much furniture. She leaned her head against the high back of the chair, and told herself that she must do better than this.

"Like a drink?" West asked.

He held out a flask, and she took it slowly and sipped—it was brandy. She wasn't used to brandy. She didn't take any more, but handed the flask back, and watched him as he screwed the cap on deliberately, and then tucked it away in his hip pocket.

"Now, what happened?" he asked, in a matter-of-fact voice.

She licked her lips, and he didn't try to force her.

"Meg—Meg telephoned me. She wanted me to take as much money as I could—here. She told me where it was. I—came, and—"

"We'd warned you not to."

"She—was frightened."

"She had reason to be. Did she say why she was frightened?"

"She said it was—a matter of—life and death."

"Well, you knew that," said West. "When are you going to grow up?"

She didn't answer.

"What happened when you arrived?"

She remembered everything vividly, and was sure that she remembered everything Latimer had said; that he had not killed the others, that he wouldn't kill anyone, and that he thought "they" would frame him. She told the story slowly, trying to keep calm; and perhaps because of the brandy or because of the manner of the two men, she felt much better when she had finished.

West nodded slowly.

"So you made him a present of the poker."

"I didn't mean—"

"Listen," said West. "You need to get some sleep and a good long rest, Miss Sharp; you've been living on your nerves for too long. Your sister isn't badly hurt; she'll be all right. I'm going to send you home."

"All—right," she said.

Peel and a constable went home with her. Peel asked the same questions as West, when they reached the flat. She gave him the same answers. Peel was quite cool and impersonal, and she felt that he was trying to catch her out in some contradiction, but she told the simple truth.

"I know; it's a bind," Roger said. "I'd rather be holding your hands in the pictures, my sweet, but I must see Margaret Sharp."

"The bold, handsome woman," said Janet.

"A modern Juno, and you ought to know the rest! Sorry, sweet. I'll get home as soon as I can."

"I won't wait up," said Janet.

Roger replaced the telephone, lit a cigarette, and scanned Peel's report and his own written report of the conversation with Georgina Sharp. Her story seemed to stand up, but there was a weakness; had she left home simply because she was frightened to stay away from her sister? Or was there a reason she hadn't yet divulged? She had personality and strong will power, and she would go her own way, daring the world to stop her. There was a lot to like about Georgina Sharp, even in her frame of mind at the house near Praed Street. But—was she a liar?

Peel's report was brief and factual; it really said there was nothing new.

Roger didn't know how much of the news had reached the press; probably most of it. If the story of Latimer's escape hit the headlines next morning, there would be another storm. He damned all politicians; they chose the worst possible time for plonking down their silly feet.

He'd almost given up hope that there would be news of Latimer. The man had gone to earth somewhere in London, and there wasn't a squeak about where. Latimer wasn't known outside his own set, and if any of those knew anything, they were putting up a strong defense.

Sloan came breezing in.

"Hallo, Handsome. Late duty?"

"I'm waiting for a call from the nursing home; I want to see Margaret Sharp as soon as she comes round."

"I hope she doesn't wait until the morning," said Sloan. "Peel's down in the canteen, looking as if a ton of bricks had fallen on him. Smithson's sitting glaring, which suggests he'll swap sides, and start a murder agency of his own. Do you think they really got as close as that to Latimer?"

Roger didn't speak.

Sloan said: "If it was Latimer, what's wrong?"

"What's right?" asked Roger. "If Latimer lifted

all that money, he wouldn't be stuck for a few pounds—unless he was afraid we should trace the lot, and he had to get some we couldn't trace to him. But it doesn't ring a bell."

"You're right it doesn't," said Sloan. "He swore to Georgina that he didn't kill anyone, and he certainly doesn't act as if he took that loose money. I can't add it up, unless—"

"There's a mystery man."

"Almost a pity Raymond Arlen was killed," Sloan said. "We'd be on to him by now. I wonder why he lied, and what he was doing. Anything else from the Newbury Police?"

"Not a cheep," said Roger, and the telephone bell rang. "Hallo?"

He listened, and said: "Fine, I'll come at once." As he put down the telephone, he said to Sloan: "Margaret Sharp's come round."

Her face was pale and her eyes enormous. She was wearing a white flannelette nightdress. Her braided hair was untidy, and her eyes had the curious brightness which sometimes comes when the pupils are very small. She lay propped up on the pillows, with a police nurse sitting in one corner of the small, drab room. On the bedside table was a small glass with a thermometer and some cotton wool in it, a carafe of water and a tumbler. The room had the sharp, penetrating smell of antiseptics. Her arms were stretched out over the bedclothes, and the sleeves of the nightdress hid everything but her long, slim hands.

She was handsome and striking, even when like this.

She looked up as Roger went in, and a flicker of

recognition crossed her face. She looked away, toward the uncurtained window, and didn't speak.

The doctor had allowed him fifteen minutes.

He drew up a high-backed chair and sat at the side of the bed, and she turned to look at him.

"What is it you want?" she asked in a toneless voice.

"I'd like to know just what happened, Miss Sharp."

"You're—that police inspector."

"Yes. And if it weren't for the police, both you and your sister might be dead."

"Might we?"

"Ralph Latimer—"

"Oh, no," she said, in the same toneless voice. "Ralph wouldn't have killed us. It was the other man."

"What other man?"

"I didn't see him very well," she said. "Ralph was in the kitchen; I was just going out. The other man came and attacked me. He put his hands round my throat." Her own hands moved to her throat, almost caressingly; she seemed too emotionless to feel any fear now. "He just squeezed and squeezed, and everything went black. It wasn't—Ralph."

"But Latimer was there?"

"Of course he was there," she said. "He was in trouble, and asked me to help him. So I went to do what I could. I suppose you want to know everything, and I don't mind helping, but you mustn't think that Ralph killed anyone. He's too—too kind."

Roger didn't speak.

"He rang me up, and I took him some chocolate and a little money. I hadn't much; it wasn't enough

161

for him to get out of the country. I pleaded with him to stay and to give himself up, but he was too frightened. He said that everyone was sure he'd killed these people, and it was a lie, he'd been—framed. I think that's the word he used."

Her monotonous voice was like that of a woman in a trance. She showed no expression, and her full, shapely lips only moved a little.

"Did he say who had framed him?"

"He said he didn't know. He was—in trouble. He was very silly; he took drugs some time ago, and sold them to some women. He said that you were after him for that; that's why he went into hiding. One of the persons he sold them to said that she would tell you. So he went into hiding, and then—then everything began to happen. He was too frightened to give himself up, and I didn't really blame him. He said that he could get out of the country; he had a false passport and everything he needed; he knew where to get some French francs, but he needed the money to buy them. He was—ill. I could tell that from looking at him. He said that he'd hardly had any food for the past few days: he'd had a few cups of coffee and a sandwich or two, that's all. He was terribly worked up."

"Do you know what he was doing at the house in Pullinger Street?"

"It belonged to a friend of his; he had a key."

"Had you ever been there before?"

"Oh, yes. I've met him there several times; it was our—trysting place." Even those words came out flatly, with no sign of emotion. "Gina was always watching me, always interfering, and I wanted to have somewhere we could meet in secret."

"You didn't tell us about that address."

"I didn't want you to find out," she said. She was

162

like a big, floppy, simple schoolgirl. "So of course I didn't tell you. I could see you thought he'd killed those people, and I was sure you were wrong. I asked him, and he swore on his heart that he knew nothing about it."

"And you believed him?"

"Of course I believed him," said Margaret Sharp. "There wasn't any reason why he should lie to me. In any case, I told him that if he didn't tell me the truth, I wouldn't help him. When he told me, I went out and telephoned Georgina and asked her to bring some more money. I didn't know whether I could rely on her."

That complaining note about Georgina kept creeping into her story.

"Yet you knew there was danger for her."

"Don't be silly; there wasn't any danger. *I* didn't know the other man would come, did I? I came away in such a hurry I could only take some chocolate. There's a café open round the corner, and I promised to go and get some food. I opened the door, and the man attacked me; I've told you about that. He was at the front door, and Ralph was in the kitchen. He was putting the kettle on: we were going to have some tea. I just don't remember anything more."

Roger said gently: "All right, Miss Sharp; all we want is the simple truth. Are you feeling all right?"

"I just feel unhappy," she said. "For poor Ralph."

"You were in love with him, weren't you?"

"I *am* in love with him," she said.

"With your brother?" asked Roger, deliberately obtuse.

She didn't answer immediately, but the only sign of shock she gave was a rounding of her big

163

eyes and a movement of her hands; neither of them amounted to much. She stared at him unblinking.

"Don't be silly," she said again. "Ralph isn't my brother. My parents adopted him, that's all. So you've found out about that," she added, with some sign of quickening interest. "I thought you would, sooner or later. I suppose you know the whole story, about his father—but if you think he's mad, *you're* crazy."

"How did you come to know about his father's madness?" asked Roger.

18

More of the Past

Margaret Sharp closed her eyes, and Roger wondered if she were going to take refuge behind pretended weariness. The police nurse shifted her position. Roger glanced at his watch; he had been here for twelve minutes, and that meant he hadn't much time left. He might get an extension from the doctor, but expected an interruption at any minute. He doubted if he could make Meg hurry if he pressed too hard, and forced himself to wait patiently.

Footsteps sounded in the passage, but a man passed.

The woman opened her eyes.

"Of course I knew all about it," she said. "He was younger than I. I can remember when he was brought to my home, just a baby of a few months. I thought he was wonderful then, and I've always thought he was wonderful. Gina couldn't understand it, but Gina's such a little fool. All she thinks about is money and getting on in the world. As if that mattered! Happiness is the only thing that matters."

"And you were happy with Ralph Latimer?"

"Not all the time, because I knew he was mixing with the wrong people. I lost touch with him for years, and only found him again by accident. That was about a year ago. I knew the whole story, you see; my mother had told me. He hadn't known anything about his past; he *thought* he was my real brother. Then something happened to make him doubt. I don't know what it was. He didn't tell me much about it. But during the years when we were separated he found out everything he could about his past—whose son he was, why he had been adopted. I knew that it worried him. I think that was one of the reasons he was so delighted when we met again. He couldn't talk about it to strangers, but he could talk to me. I reassured him, of course. I told him he needn't worry about heredity; all he needed to worry about was getting out of the hands of these bad people.

"He owed them a lot of money; that was the trouble.

"I just had to help him, and so I took our money —that is, Gina's and mine. I knew Gina would never understand what I felt for Ralph; she just has the normal reactions. She'd have thought that his mind was unreliable, and so I couldn't tell her. Ralph was able to pay off everything he owed, thanks to me, and then—this woman blackmailed him."

"Do you know the woman?"

"No," said Margaret Sharp.

"Didn't he mention her—even her Christian name?"

"No."

"You're sure he was being blackmailed."

"He told me so," she said, simply. "And then

these dreadful murders started, and he was frightened. He saw in a moment what everyone would think—that he wasn't sane, had homicidal tendencies, like his father. I just *had* to help him. I knew people would call me foolish, but I didn't worry about that. Did—did Gina give him the money?"

"Yes."

For the first time, her eyes brightened.

"Oh, that's good! He'll get away!"

"Do you know where he was going?"

"Somewhere in France, he said. He had a false passport—there isn't much you can teach Ralph." She was proud.

"Did he mention any town or city? Paris, for instance?"

"No," she said. "He said that the less I knew about it the better; but he promised to get in touch with me when everything had blown over, so that I could go and join him. I expect he'll find a way of writing safely. Once he had the money, he was quite sure that he would be all right. He speaks French like a native," she added, still proudly.

There were more footsteps in the passage outside; and this time the doctor opened the door.

"I don't suppose you'll ever find him," said Margaret Sharp.

"She was unconscious for several hours," Roger said to the doctor. "Would the strangling have affected her like that?"

"No," said the doctor. "She was drugged. Morphia, almost for certain. It wasn't a big dose—just enough to send her off. She'll be as right as rain in the morning, and then you can question her as much as you like."

*　　　*　　　*

The West boys had a kind of sixth sense where their father was concerned, and knew those occasions when he was hardly aware of their existence. Led by Scoopy, they meekly left the breakfast table next morning, and put on their caps and coats, for school. It was overcast and cold, with a promise of rain. Janet stood up when she knew that the boys were ready, but didn't go out immediately. She stood looking down at Roger, who was running through the third of several daily papers. The headlines were about Latimer's escape. He was scowling as he buttered some toast and piled on the marmalade. She knew that he was hardly aware of her existence.

Suddenly he thrust the newspaper away, and grinned up at her.

"Hallo! You here?"

"Still waiting for you," said Janet. "Darling, don't take any notice of that nonsense. You'd think they'd get tired of baiting the Yard."

"Oh, I don't know—Latimer's dodged us twice when we ought to have caught him. Can't expect much mercy from Fleet Street. Chatworth will be in a hell of a mood this morning." He forced a laugh. "I'd better get off—are the boys ready?"

Richard burst into the room.

"Daddy-could-you-take-us-to-school-in-the-car?"

"*I* wanted to ask!" cried Scoopy, hurtling along the passage, bumping into Richard and sending him forward unsteadily. But Richard, in his triumph, was unperturbed.

"Could you, Daddy?"

"Yes!"

"Oh, good."

"Really?" asked Scoopy, as if he knew this wasn't

in tune with the breakfast-table mood. "Can I sit in the front?"

"I asked first!" flashed Richard.

"No, you didn't; I—"

"Who sat in the front last time?" asked Janet.

"Scoopy did!"

"Richard did!"

Roger took a penny from his pocket.

"We'll toss for it," he said. "Your call, Fish."

Richard's big eyes followed the toss of the coin, Scoopy held his breath, and as Roger caught the coin, Richard squeaked: "Heads—no, *tails.*"

Roger kept the penny covered.

"Tails?"

"Yes," said Richard, and his thumb went to his mouth.

Roger held out his hand, and the boys pressed forward, as he took the covering hand away slowly. It was heads.

"I've won!" cried Scoopy, and turned and rushed out, to make sure that he couldn't be dispossessed of the fruits of victory.

Richard's great eyes contemplated Roger for several seconds, while Janet stood with a hand on Roger's shoulder. Then, with great deliberation, Richard said: "I *really* wanted heads."

"Then next time say exactly what you want," said Roger. "Off with you."

Richard ran.

Janet placed her hands on either side of Roger's face.

"Darling."

"Hm-hm?"

"Do you wish you were single?"

Roger started. "What on earth are you talking about?"

"I often wonder," said Janet, half seriously. "You've so much on your mind, you want to think about nothing but Latimer; you really had to make an effort to pay the boys a little attention, didn't you?"

"Well, I made it," said Roger, and took her wrists. He looked upward, so that her face appeared upside down. "I love you."

"I wonder."

"Listen!" said Roger. "Don't you start!"

"All detectives ought to be single," said Janet.

"All detectives' wives ought to be sensible," said Roger, "and *you* ought to be used to it by now."

He took her hands away and stood up.

The car horn sounded, outside, and Richard's treble voice piped: "Don't, Scoopy!"

The horn sounded again.

Roger put his arms round Janet, and said: "My sweet, if I hadn't a wife to love and boys to bellow at occasionally, I'd go crazy. Ten minutes with you is like a long drink on a hot day."

He kissed her.

A few minutes later, driving along the King's Road toward the school, he was smiling to himself and picturing Janet's face, upside down to him. Even after he'd dropped the boys, he was still smiling, and thinking more of home than of the case. Nearing the Yard he began to think of Latimer and the headlines about his latest escape, and the advent of the mystery man; but he still smiled. There was one way to get everything out of his mind when it was clouded, as it was over this affair; the one way was at home.

He pulled up in the Yard, chuckled, and climbed out.

Superintendent Abbott, a tall and gloomy-looking man not renowned for his sense of humor, was walking across from Cannon Row.

"You can't have read this morning's papers, West."

"Only three of them," said Roger. "After our blood, aren't they?"

"After *your* blood."

"Sink or swim together," said Roger, and chuckled again. "Latimer won't have a much longer run. Been to the office yet?"

"No."

"If anything that matters were in, I'd have heard about it," said Roger.

He was still blithe as he went upstairs. Sloan was already in his shirt sleeves, but hadn't yet unloosened his collar and tie. It was ten minutes past nine, and Roger lit a cigarette and skimmed through other newspapers which were folded in a neat pile on his desk. The *Daily Cry* was almost venomous in its attack on the carelessness which had allowed Latimer to escape a second time.

"What's got into you?" asked Sloan, looking at him curiously. "Come into a fortune, or do you know where Latimer is?"

"Not yet. Nothing in?"

"Absolutely nothing. Ports and airports were all watched, no one remotely like Latimer left the country after you'd got Meg Sharp's story about that faked passport. I doubt if he had time to get out before that, but I'm checking for passengers who bought their tickets at the last moment. As you ordered! I'm also having a stab at all the sources of black-market francs, to see if he'd made contact. Not that I expect much from that." Sloan sat on the corner of Roger's desk, and smoothed down his thick, wiry fair hair. "Why so cheerful?"

"Those boys of mine."

"Oh, I see," said Sloan. "Well, don't tell the A.C., or he'll ask if you mean to bring them in to help you. That'll be his mood this morning."

"It'll pass." Roger tossed the newspapers aside. There was a pile of reports, inches high. "Been through these?"

"Yes. I had Peel in, to help sort them out. He was here first."

"Our Jim's very anxious to justify himself," said Roger. "Pity things went wrong last night; he and Smithson deserve a good break. What do you make of things?"

Sloan said: "One fact sticks out a mile."

Roger nodded.

"Everything we hear about Latimer is in flat contradiction to what we know about the murderer," said Sloan. "You can't have missed that."

"I haven't, Bill."

"Darned if I know what to make of it," Sloan grumbled. "He's surely hard up, or he wouldn't have had both women take him money. He might have hoped that Meg would get her hands on another hundred; but if he had several hundred, he wouldn't take risks for a few pounds. According to her, he was hungry, too—and that ties up with his statement to Georgina. In fact, it all ties up."

"And leaves us what?"

Sloan stood up. "This damned mystery man."

"How we need a missing Raymond Arlen, instead of a dead one," said Roger. "No remote chance of mistaken identity over Raymond Arlen's body, is there?"

"No."

"Pity. He's our other mystery. Everything else

seems answered, except what he was doing when he didn't get home late that night, and—"

"Good Lord!" exclaimed Sloan.

"Now what?"

"I didn't tell you—it's there, though. Came in this morning. Raymond Arlen didn't make any business calls in North Wales. The customers he usually saw there haven't seen him for a month. He certainly didn't go away on a business trip."

Roger said: "Well, well!"

"I suppose—" began Sloan, and hesitated.

"Yes, he could have killed Wilfred Arlen and Lionel Bennett, and he could have attacked Mrs. Drew; but he certainly wasn't about last night," said Roger.

"Even I can see that. But is it possible that Latimer did the attacking last night, for some reason we don't yet know? And that Arlen did the murders in order to—"

Roger grinned. "Yes?"

"That's where I come to a full stop," confessed Sloan.

Roger said: "Try it this way, Bill. Raymond Arlen, for some reason as yet unknown, started to get rid of some of his relatives. He then came to see us, and drew attention to his own likeness to Latimer. He then told us of Arnold, the son of the insane Uncle Simon. Add that all up, and you have the possibility that he was the killer, turning our attention to a possible homicidal maniac. If that happened, it wasn't so bad, but—who killed Raymond Arlen?"

Sloan said: "The shots were fired at close quarters; they *could* have been self-inflicted. I suppose the Newbury people haven't slipped up in looking for the revolver."

"Automatic pistol. No, they wouldn't have to look far—you know they haven't slipped up. We can accept the possibility that Raymond did the first murders and the attack on Mrs. Drew, but we haven't the answer to his murder, unless Latimer discovered what he was doing. Latimer's been very insistent that he was being framed. His story of being scared because of the drug business, and then getting into a panic because everyone thought he'd killed Wilfred and Lionel, isn't all that strong. On the other hand, if he killed Raymond Arlen because Arlen was framing him, then we'd have a pretty strong motive. What's the snag?"

Sloan pondered, and then said: "The same gun was used."

"That's it. Well, we could invent another possibility," said Roger. "That Raymond Arlen and Latimer met, that they had a quarrel, that Latimer took Raymond's gun—that would explain away one puzzle. I suppose I could take this along to the A.C. and make out quite a case for it. We'd first have to establish that Latimer and Raymond Arlen knew each other. If we did that, we might catch Latimer and find that he's a self-defense case— would plead not guilty to the first jobs, and self-defense in the other. That would work out nicely, wouldn't it?"

Sloan said: "You've tied it all up pretty neatly. I didn't hear anything about this yesterday."

"An empty mind fills up quickest," said Roger, "and mine was emptied for ten minutes this morning." He laughed. "I won't tell Chatworth that, either! What do you think of the build-up?"

"It *seems* to answer everything."

"Except Margaret Sharp and her possible hidden motives and secrets," said Roger. "And there's the

174

big gap—did Raymond Arlen know Latimer? What was he lying about?"

"You're pretty sure this is the answer, aren't you?"

"Not yet, but it could be. Bill, let's try a new tack. You take some time off, see Raymond Arlen's employers, find out how he was doing. Then have a dig at the Bennetts, and find out if there was any reason, except silly shame, why they hushed up the history of Simon Arlen. Your best way will be through Lionel Bennett's solicitors. Go deep."

Sloan nodded.

"Anything from Birmingham, and the only known surviving blood relations?" asked Roger briskly.

"Not much. Both Arthur and Ernest Bennett were watched by the Birmingham people last night; there was a special guard at dusk and during the night. Nothing happened. Neither of them stirred out of their homes after dusk. I can't say I blame them! The Newbury people say that Mrs. Raymond hasn't added anything. Nor has Mrs. Drew, who's come round—she didn't recognize the man who shot her. Muriel Arlen is up and about again, and her son's back home."

"Oh," said Roger. "I suppose we haven't taken too much for granted with her."

"Such as?"

"That Latimer was just a boy friend. All right, lover. I'd say she was just as much in love with Latimer as Meg Sharp."

"Whichever way you look at it, Latimer was a bounder," said Sloan. "But there seem to be two of him—or rather two versions of the same man. To Mrs. Muriel Arlen he was a cultured type, couldn't have been better, and yet—"

"I think I'll have another talk with her," Roger said. "But I want to be present when Georgina and Margaret Sharp have their reunion. Ring me at Merrick Street, will you?"

The wizened-looking man servant at Merrick Street opened the door. He took Roger into the drawing room, with its restful charm. Roger heard a boy's voice, sounding bright enough; so Dennis had not succumbed to the shock. There were footsteps, and Mrs. Arlen came in. Roger caught a glimpse of the boy, peering at him; he was probably eager to set eyes on a man from Scotland Yard.

Mrs. Arlen closed the door.

"Good morning, Mr. West."

"I'm sorry to worry you again," Roger said formally, "but we're still looking for Latimer, as you know."

"I've read everything about it," said Mrs. Arlen. "Please sit down." She sat opposite him. Her color was better; she looked too bright about the eyes, and was obviously restless, but she was in much better shape than when he had seen her before. Her glance was calm and direct. "You will think I am foolish, but I feel quite sure that Ralph did not commit those murders. It is *not* the kind of thing he would do."

So many people, even with intelligence, seemed to think that you could tell a murderer simply by looking at him.

"I hope you're right; but why doesn't he come into the open?" Roger asked mildly.

"I can believe that he would be frightened into hiding," said the woman. "After all, the newspapers make it quite clear that he is suspected of the murders. I am seriously thinking of asking for legal advice, Mr. West."

"Oh?"

"It amounts to libel. No man should be judged until he's found guilty."

Roger said: "No. I don't think the papers have gone too far yet; they've stated the simple truth—that we're looking for him, and have twice missed him near the scene of—"

"How can you be sure he was the man you failed to catch?"

"We've some evidence." Roger was still mild; judged that she would, if necessary, fly to the defense of Latimer; marveled that she should feel like this—and that Meg Sharp should have equal faith in the man. Latimer had qualities which didn't show in most of his record. "Have you any idea where he is, Mrs. Arlen?"

"I have not!"

"Or where he might be?"

"You or your colleagues have asked me that so often that I shall soon think that I am branded a liar," she said coldly.

"Women in love have been known to lie."

She flushed, and made as if to stand up, then dropped back into her chair.

"I do not know where he is; I have no idea where he might be found. As far as I am aware, he had only one address, and I have told you about it."

"Did you know that he was a relation of your husband?"

"I have read suggestions in the newspapers. I am not convinced that it's true."

Roger said: "I see," and stood up.

If she were lying, she did it well. He bowed distantly, and went out, but did not think that he had worried her. He let himself out by the front door, and as he stepped onto the porch, saw the boy, Dennis. He was tall for his age, very pale, but starry-eyed. There was no doubt of his eagerness to meet a man from the Yard.

"Hallo," said Roger. "So you're Dennis."

"Yes, *you're* Chief Inspector West."

"That's right."

Dennis licked his lips. "Have you—" He broke off.

"Yes?"

"Have you found that man who killed my father?"

"We will, old chap," said Roger.

"I'd like to *kick* him," said Dennis. "I hate him. I—"

"Dennis!" His mother called from the door.

"Oh, all right," said Dennis, "I'm coming." He gulped, and looked at Roger. "Good-by, sir."

He offered his hand, and Roger gripped it firmly. The woman didn't speak.

If Latimer were the killer, her son hated the man she loved; and she must realize that whether he was a killer or not, Latimer was bad. What frame of mind was she in? If she had an opportunity to help Latimer, would she take it?

He sat at the wheel of his car, pondering. A constable was on the other side of the road, a Divisional man whose job was to watch the house. He recognized Roger and nodded, but didn't come across.

Yes, she'd help Latimer, as readily as Meg Sharp would. She was already defiant, thinking in terms of defending the man. What had Latimer got, to cause such loyalty?

At the Yard he said to Sloan: "I think we'll have

one of our men at Merrick Street, Bill; we don't want Latimer to get his next lump of money from Muriel Arlen."

"Like *that*, is it?"

"It wouldn't surprise me," said Roger. He dropped into his chair. "Nice job—all we can do now is wait until we find Latimer, except for that reunion of Sharps. When's Meg coming out of the nursing home?"

"In half an hour, in one of our cars. Chatworth wants to see—"

"Tell him I'm at Middleton Street," said Roger.

Peel was outside Number 122.

"Nothing fresh," he said.

"Seen Georgina this morning?"

"No."

Ten minutes later a police car drew up and Margaret Sharp stepped out; the driver tried to help her, but she shook off his hand. She looked regal and pale.

Roger waited five minutes, then went into the house, and stood at the foot of the stairs, listening. After a moment or two he went farther up. He heard a shout, as if someone were angry; it didn't surprise him. When he reached the Sharps' landing he could hear the voices more clearly; they were going at each other hammer and tongs. He stood with his ear close to the door, but couldn't catch the words, and couldn't see anything through the keyhole, except a closed door. He tried the handle, but it was locked. He took out his knife, which had a pick-lock blade, twisted the blade in the lock, heard the faint click as it opened. He pushed the door gently, and heard Meg Sharp scream:

"You always hated him—you'd like to see him dead!"

"Meg—"

"You'd like to see him hanged!" screeched Margaret Sharp. "Do you think I can't tell? Why? That's what I'd like to know. You make me sick! You sit around and do nothing, go and stare out of the window while that policeman makes cow eyes at you. You're—you're just a nasty little tart. *I'm* not staying here any longer."

"Meg, don't be silly. I don't want him hanged, I just want to make sure that you're not hurt any more than you have been. I tried to help—"

"Tried to help! You little liar! You brought the police to the house, didn't you? You promised you'd come alone, but you had to bring that sloppy policeman—you can't move a step without him. Well, I'm not sacrificing my Ralph to a little slut like *you*. He's worth ten of you. He never liked you —always said there was something beastly about a woman sitting *naked* in front of a man while he painted her, and that's true. You're a slut!"

"Meg, be quiet!" Anger was rising in Georgina's voice.

"I won't be quiet!"

"You're tired, you're not yourself, or—"

"*I'm* all right; I'm just beginning to see the truth about you. You with your cooing voice and your pretty smile and your sickening lies—you don't want to help me; you never have wanted to help me. Never! And now you've tried to set the police onto Ralph. I'm glad he escaped; I knew he would. The police are fools. Fools, fools, fools! They even think he killed those people, and he didn't! Do you hear me?"

Georgina said: "Yes, I can hear you—so can the

people in the street, I should think. Of course he killed them. You've been a blind fool, and now—"

There was a gasp—then a thud, a slap, and the sound of a scuffle. Roger opened the door an inch, and looked inside. Meg Sharp was standing over her sister, who was bending back against a chair, trying to fend her off; and Meg was a much bigger woman. She struck again—and then gasped and drew back, and Roger just saw Georgina's hand, clenched, coming away from the older woman's stomach; a man couldn't have hit more effectively.

Meg staggered away.

Georgina said: "You must be mad. To ask me for more money now, just for you to hand over to him! And you must be mad, to keep any secrets from the police. You know where he's gone. Don't you? You know where he's gone."

19

Trap

There was a moment of utter silence.

Roger drew back, so that he couldn't be seen, then heard Meg's thin, hissing intake of breath, followed by a swift movement.

Georgina cried: "Meg!" and there was fear in her voice.

Roger shouted: "Stop that!" and flung the door open. He saw Meg with a big stone ornament in her hand, bringing it down toward Georgina's fore-head. Georgina tried to dodge, but came up against the chair. Roger leaped. The shout had dis-tracted the bigger woman's attention, she half turned, and the ornament caught Georgina on the shoulder. Meg started to strike again. Roger reached her, and gripped her arm, and she strug-gled wildly. She dropped the ornament, and it caught him on the side of the head. She wrenched herself free, and ran screaming toward the door. He reached it just in front of her. She swung round and ran into one of the other rooms, slamming the door after her; the key turned in the lock. She was still screaming.

Georgina, white-faced, said: "She'll kill herself."

Roger reached the other door, put his shoulder to it, and pushed. It creaked. He thudded against it again, and the door gave way.

In the room beyond, Meg Sharp was lying face downward on a bed, sobbing, clutching at the bed-clothes. She didn't look round, didn't seem to know that he had forced the door.

Peel came rushing in.

"What's on? I heard—"

He broke off, at the sight of Georgina rubbing her shoulder, and Roger looking at Meg, from the door.

"All right," Roger said.

He withdrew, and left the door ajar.

Georgina went across to it.

"She'll do something drastic," she said. "She mustn't be left alone."

"She doesn't look like a suicide to me," Roger said heavily. "But go and make sure, Peel."

Peel went in and closed the door.

Georgina was rubbing her left shoulder gingerly. Her hair was disheveled and there was a scratch on her nose; a tiny globule of blood showed on it. She looked tired, too, and walked across to a chair and dropped into it. The ornament was at her feet —a big draped figure carved from a slab of mar-ble. Georgina pushed it farther away with her toe. Even like that, she couldn't conceal the natural grace of her body.

"How did you get in?"

"I heard the shouting and forced the lock."

"That's just as well for me," said Georgina. "I wouldn't have believed she could act like it. What a fool she is! Can't you—help? If you find Latimer and prove what he's done, I might be able to do something with her."

"Why not let her work out her own salvation?" asked Roger.

Georgina shrugged.

"It's become a habit to look after her. She needs help now, if ever she did."

"And you'll help?"

"As much as I can. I won't try to fool you again, if that's what you mean."

"How did the quarrel start?"

"She hadn't been home five minutes before she asked me if I could lend her a hundred pounds," said Georgina. "I've been putting some money aside, since I discovered how generous Meg was with our joint funds, and she knows that. She said she felt ill and wanted to go away for a holiday, but I could see through it as easily as I can see through that window. She knows where he is, and still wants to help him. What *has* got into her?"

Roger said: "And it's out of character?"

"You mean this screaming violence? Oh, yes. Everything's out of character. I've always told you, haven't I, that she's never gone on with any other man? She's always broken the association. Yet he seems to have taken possession of her, body and soul. She seems so unreal; it's almost as if she's acting a part. If you'd heard the pathetic way she asked me for that money—"

She broke off.

Roger murmured: "She might try again, when she's cooled down."

"I suppose so. She won't get it. She seems ready to do anything for him; doesn't mind humiliating herself, doesn't mind what difficulties it makes for her. I warned her that she would find herself in prison if she weren't careful, and that really started her going."

"If she wants money for him, she either knows where he is, or has arranged another meeting," said Roger.

"Yes," she said. "I can see that, and I'm not a detective." That was a welcome flash of humor, suggesting that she was beginning to recover her balance. "Can't you catch him, and get it over?"

"You might be able to help."

"Oh, no," said Georgina. "I've interfered too much already."

"This would be simple. Let her have what money she wants."

Georgina stared. *"What?"*

"Let her have the money. She'll have to take or send it to him. I can have her watched, letters can be opened, she can be followed everywhere—we won't lose her again now we know that she might try to dodge us. And if she led us to Latimer, then it would all be over bar shouting."

Georgina didn't speak.

"Being loyal to your sister doesn't mean being loyal to Latimer," Roger said.

"It's a—mean trick."

"It's a possible way of helping her."

"I suppose it is," said Georgina. "Perhaps you're right; but I hate the thought of being a decoy. If she ever found out—"

"She'd live to thank you."

"I wonder," said Georgina, heavily. "There are times when I wonder whether I know Meg as well as I thought I did. She certainly isn't the Meg I've always known." She rubbed her shoulder again, and forced a smile. "I suppose you think I owe you some help."

185

"You owe this to yourself."

"Oh, all right," said Georgina. "I'll play. But don't slip up this time, Mister Detective; I'm getting tired of it—another quarrel like that with Meg, and I think I should fade out from sheer fright. Do you—know—" She hesitated, caught her breath, then went on: "She really meant to—"

She broke off.

Roger said: "She really meant to kill you; she was in a murderous rage all right. Be careful."

"I'll be all right now I know what to expect," said Georgina heavily. "In any case I'm going to give her the money, aren't I?" Her lips twisted. "And how shall I tell you, if she gets it?"

"I'll have the flat watched—you won't necessarily know who's watching. Give a signal at the window. Something quite simple—go to it with your back against it and raise your hand to your head."

She laughed.

"Try it out," said Roger.

She stood up, smiling as if she thought it were foolish, backed slowly to the window, and put a hand to the back of her head in another pose that was beauty itself. In spite of her paleness, her complexion was lovely; and her eyes glowed. He could easily understand Peel or anyone else falling in love with her.

"Will that do?"

"Fine," said Roger. "Remember to leave the curtains open, at night."

Georgina said: "Be careful with her, won't you? She isn't herself; it's a kind of illness."

"I'll be careful," Roger promised.

He went downstairs with Peel, who somehow avoided looking back over his shoulder as Georgina closed the door on them. In the street, Peel rubbed the side of his chin and said ruefully: "It's a good thing you went in."

"You weren't so far away yourself," said Roger. "I'm giving Georgina a chance to prove that she wants to help."

"How?" Peel was eager.

Roger explained....

"And I'll take over part of the job myself. You stay for the rest of the day, I'll relieve you tonight. We'll want another man with us, and a car handy."

Peel said: "Look here, I—"

"Yes?"

"It's most likely to happen after dark, if it happens. Let me be on the job with you."

Roger said: "All right."

Nothing was reported during the day, except that Georgina went out for an hour early in the afternoon, did some shopping, and went straight back. One of her calls was at Lloyds Bank. The others were at the usual shops she dealt with. She had been closely watched, and there was no indication that she had passed on a substantial amount of money to anyone.

Roger took up duty at seven o'clock.

He had plenty to brood over. A peevish Chatworth, whose reproaches about the man's escape the previous night were worse than his earlier aggressiveness. The evening newspapers kept up the campaign of criticism, one of them stronger than any of the morning papers. The avalanche had started to get under the skin of the men at the Yard. Sloan had not yet obtained much information about the Arlens and the Bennetts, except that Raymond Arlen had been highly regarded by his employers, and earned never less than two thousand pounds a year. He had only a hundred or so in the Bank, and certainly lived up to his income.

Peel was already in Middleton Street.

"You take the far end, I'll take this," said Roger. "If she comes out, work exactly as you did with Smithson—I'll trail her on foot; you drive the car to pick me up. And have the radio working overtime; let the Yard know everywhere we go."

"I'm not going to slip up again," Peel said. "Think she'll come?"

They looked up at the lighted and uncurtained window of the front room at the flat. Roger didn't answer. Now and again a shadow appeared at the window, and once they saw Meg's back. But an hour passed, and darkness fell, and there was no warning sign.

Roger lit his fourth cigarette.

He was halfway through it when he saw Georgina at the window. She glanced out, then turned around. Her hand went to the back of her head.

20

Chase

Nothing else happened.

Georgina stayed at the window for several seconds, but did not look round again. Roger, keyed up, waited for the front door to open, and it remained closed. He could see the sidelights of Peel's car farther along the street; the engine hummed—a sign of expectancy—but still the door remained closed.

Roger strained his ears to catch any sound of a police whistle from the back of the houses; there was none. The men on duty there wouldn't be sleeping on their jobs. He began to walk toward Number 122, and peered across at it; there was no doubt that the door had been closed.

A clock struck nine, not far away.

Peel switched off the engine of his car, and Roger joined him; the window was down.

"She's been twenty minutes," Peel said. "I thought she'd have come running out as soon as she got her hand on the cash."

"She isn't going to try the same trick twice," Roger said. "I think we may have underestimated

189

Meg. Get on the other side of the road, will you—facing this way?"

He pointed toward a corner, beyond which was the High Street.

Peel didn't ask questions, but obeyed.

Roger crossed to the other side of the street, and stood a few yards from the front door. Peel's car was now in its new position; only the rear light and the dark outline of the little car showed. Another car turned into the street, from behind both Roger and Peel, and came along swiftly. Roger was staring at the door, keyed up, as he had been from the moment he had spoken to Peel.

The car squealed to a standstill.

The door of Number 122 opened.

Roger caught a glimpse of a woman at the wheel of the car which had just stopped, and of Meg Sharp, rushing toward the car. He flattened himself against the side of a house, anxious not to be seen. If he showed himself now, they would never lead him to Latimer.

The door alongside the driver was open. The big woman squeezed herself inside, moving with surprising speed, and slamming the door as the car started off. It hadn't stood still for thirty seconds. As it moved, Roger sprinted. He could not hear Peel's car start up, the engine of the other was making too much noise. It reached the corner as Roger sat next to Peel, who sent his car roaring toward the corner.

The first car turned left—into the High Street.

As Peel reached it, a bus was swinging toward them. Peel trod on the accelerator, the car shot forward, and someone on the pavement screamed. The bus driver jammed on his brakes and the bus swerved. A motorcyclist, coming in the other direction, swung toward the curb as Peel turned, and mounted it. Another woman screamed, a policeman appeared in the light of another car, waving wildly.

"Nice work," Roger said.

Peel slid between two more cars, cutting in dangerously. The women's small car was close to them now; it was possible that the women knew they had been followed. Peel slackened pace. A car drew alongside, with a policeman standing on the running board, and it started to cut in.

"C.I.D.," called Roger.

The policeman stopped, the car swerved out of Peel's way, and he went on. The first car swung round to the left. It went toward Notting Hill Gate.

Peel had switched on the radio.

Roger grabbed it.

"Chief Inspector West, calling Scotland Yard. Can you hear me?"

"Yard answering. We can hear you."

"Margaret Sharp is going up Church Street with another woman in black or dark blue Austin 12 saloon car, registration number BX 241B. Alert all patrol cars and all duty forces. Report progress of car back to me. Message ends. Repeat please."

The report came back, word perfect.

"All right," Roger said to Peel. "Relax."

The smaller car passed out of sight; several others were between them and the women now. After the first two minutes there was a call from the Yard. A patrol car had passed the women near the Bayswater Road. Another reported it in the Bayswater Road. There was a silence of several minutes, then came a report that it had turned into Leinster Gardens. Another pause, then several more reports. The car was obviously taking a roundabout route; the driver was trying to make sure that she wasn't followed.

Peel said: "They can't dodge this time."

"Our Meg believes in miracles," said Roger.

"Recognize the other woman?"

"No, but it wasn't Georgina."

Peel grunted. "Think it might have been Mrs. Arlen?"

"I don't know."

"It wouldn't surprise *me*," said Peel.

"It would me."

Peel started to ask why, and there was another message from a patrol car near Paddington Station. Roger sat tensely, half expecting to be told that they had gone to the station, trying to remember what trains left about this time; they might have made a wild dive to catch a certain train; there were local as well as long-distance lines from Paddington. Peel was in the street where the car had last been reported, still driving with reckless skill.

"*Austin BX 241B now in Edgware Road,*" came a message.

Roger relaxed. "Not the station, anyhow."

"I've just had a nasty thought," said Peel.

"What?"

"She might have stopped and let Meg get off; that would fool us."

"Be cheerful," said Roger.

But it could have happened.

"*Yard calling Chief Inspector West. Austin BX 241B now in Oxford Street, heading toward the City.*"

"Soho?" suggested Peel. "He turned up there once, remember. May have a hideout there."

"Maybe."

Peel said: "What makes you doubt if it's Mrs. Arlen?"

Roger laughed. "She has plenty of money; she wouldn't need to get a hundred pounds from the Sharps to help her Ralph along."

"Sorry," grunted Peel. "I'm not myself."

"On the other hand, she might just have arranged to go and see her Ralph," said Roger. "The women could be in the rescue attempt together; but if you can think of anything less likely, I'll resign."

"Or course not."

"*Yard calling Chief Inspector West. Austin BX 241B now in Charing Cross Road, seen to turn right into . . .*"

"Soho!" exclaimed Peel.

They were no more than a hundred yards from Charing Cross Road. Peel cut into a side street, taking a chance, made several wide turns, and ran into Dean Street. Fifty yards along another car was pulling into the curb; it looked about the size of the wanted Austin. A woman got out, and was just visible in the light from a café; she was a massive, dark lump who disappeared into a doorway. The car stopped only just long enough for her to get out.

"Now we've got 'em!" crowed Peel.

"*Hold it. Chief Inspector West calling. Passenger has left Austin BX 241B in Dean Street. Send patrols to Dean Street, block each end and all side turnings. Detail one patrol car to follow Austin to destination. Can you hear me?*"

"*Message received.*"

Peel pulled into the side of the road about twenty yards from the doorway into which the woman had disappeared. Another police patrol car turned into the street. Peel jumped into the road, to stop it; Roger went along past the small shops, the cafés, the boarded-up debris of what had once been shops. All the doors were closed. He pushed each one. The café light was only a few doors away, and he had seen Meg Sharp against that; she certainly had gone past it. He pushed another door, and it creaked open.

He stopped.

Peel came up.

"Anything?"

"The door was open, she didn't have time to use a key," Roger said. "But she may have slammed it and put me off. Anyhow, she's around here. Have you detailed the others?"

"They'll seal the place up." Peel's voice was deep with satisfaction. "Hunt nearly over, Roger."

Roger said: "Don't you be too sure. I wish I had a gun."

Peel didn't speak.

They stepped inside the narrow passage which led from the open door. Darkness and silence met them. There was no certainty that this was the right place. They stood and listened, and all they could hear was footsteps approaching outside; there was no sound above, no murmur of voices.

They reached the first landing, and Roger shone his torch. Its light fell upon the only door. It had the name of a firm on it, and there were two Yale locks.

"Better stay here, Jim."

Peel grunted.

Roger went up the next flight of wooden stairs. They creaked so loudly that it was almost certain that they would be heard above. He saw a glimmer of light above him, coming from the top or the

194

sides of a door. At the next landing he saw the outline of the door against a slight filtering of light, and then the light went out.

Peel's whisper floated up.

"Anything?"

Roger didn't answer. There were fresh sounds, as if men had stepped stealthily into the passage downstairs. Creaking followed; they were coming up, Peel was probably in the lead. Roger tried the handle of the door, but it was locked; his torchlight showed a Yale, and he couldn't open that with a pick-lock. He could open it if he had the right materials; one of the patrol-car men might have some cracksmen's implements.

Peel breathed almost into his ear.

"This it?"

"Are the other places well watched?"

"We've got six cars outside, they say."

"Good." Roger hesitated, then thumped on the door with the side of his clenched fist. The noise sounded very loud. He heard nothing else, and kicked the door, and then called clearly: *"Open in the name of the law!"*

There were moments when the stock phrase was impressive. There had been someone in here; they could certainly hear what he said. If he were wrong in his guess, then the door would be opened.

There was silence.

Roger said: "I think we're home. One of you go down, check the back of this place, and have it surrounded. Make sure all exits from the street are blocked, too, and remind everyone that he's probably armed."

A man went off.

"Come on," said Roger. "Let's see how strong you are."

195

They put their combined weight against the door, and it groaned and sagged. They heaved again, grunting; there was an explosive crack, and the door swung inward. Roger pitched forward, Peel flung himself to one side, each expecting a shot; there was none. Light came from another door across the room they'd entered—from a wide gap at one side.

This was a sitting room, with old armchairs, couches, low tables, cheap wallpaper, a general air of dilapidation and cheapness. Peel switched on the light, which showed the room in all its tawdry gloom. But they didn't worry about the tawdriness. Two more men joined them as they reached the other door.

Roger spoke over his shoulder.

"Sure everything's watched at the back?"

"Yes, sir," said one of the men. "They can't get away. Better have this, sir."

The man held an axe.

Roger took it. "Thanks." He was breathing normally again, and raised his voice. "Latimer, it's no use—open the door."

No one replied.

Roger said: "Open in the name of the law," and went forward again; this time the phrase seemed like a cliché, an empty mockery. Why? He'd called to Latimer, and couldn't be sure that Latimer was inside; couldn't be absolutely sure that Meg Sharp was. That swiftly moving figure, visible only for a moment, might have been someone else; he might find himself fooled again.

He smashed at a panel of the door, near the handle, and stood aside. His men stood by the wall, Peel nearest; all of them were thinking of the close-quarters shooting which had started this affair. There was a sound now, as if someone were panting.

Roger struck again, and levered the axe; wood splintered, and there was room to put his hand through. He didn't fancy it, but moved quickly. He had to grope for the key, expected a bullet or a weapon smashing against his fingers; it didn't come. He turned the key and moved aside as the door swung open a few inches.

"Now don't play the fool," he said, and kicked the door wide open.

He saw Margaret Sharp, and relief surged through him. She was standing a few feet out from a corner, hands raised in front of her breast, braided hair loose, mouth open.

"Keep away!" she gasped. "Keep away!"

"Now don't be silly," said Roger.

Was Latimer hiding behind her? She was big enough to conceal him. The man wasn't in sight. Roger edged in, making sure that the room was empty except for that corner. Peel followed him, and went slowly toward a window, and the woman backed, as if to hide whoever was behind her. Roger darted to one side; she moved to block his path, and he swung round again

There was no one in the corner.

Peel flung up the window, and called down.

"Anyone seen him?"

The answer came promptly: "No."

There was one other door, which was closed. It was opposite the window. Roger knew the type of building well enough to be sure it was a tiny kitchen, with little room; probably there would be a window in it. He walked across as Meg Sharp flung herself at him. The waiting C.I.D. men grabbed her arms; she struggled and cried, but couldn't free herself. Roger didn't glance round, but there was a picture of her face in his mind's eye: the open mouth and terrified eyes, as if she were looking at the end of the world. Now she was sobbing, wildly and unnaturally.

He called: "Latimer, come out."

There was no answer; he wondered again if they were fooling him, if he would find Latimer beyond this door. He kicked it; it was more solid than the others. He smashed at it with the axe, wrenching the blade out after each heavy blow, and at last the door swung open. He stepped to one side. He was making almost a habit of this, and this time he was slower; he didn't expect a bullet.

He didn't get one.

The little room beyond was in darkness, but a breeze came soft on his face; a window was open.

"Give it up, Latimer," he said in an easy voice. "You're not doing yourself any good like this."

He moved forward, trying to see into the room. The light from this was sufficient to show him a sink, the open window, a plate rack and some crockery; if Latimer were in here, he was hiding behind the door. Roger pushed it, and it banged against the wall and swung slowly toward him again.

There was no cupboard, no possible hiding place.

He stepped toward the window.

From outside a man shouted: "Look out! He's got a gun!"

21

Capture

Roger stood close to the side of the window, peering out. There were lights outside, and more came on, filling the night with a yellow glow. Just within range, he saw uniformed policemen and plainclothes men taking shelter behind walls, all staring upward. The lights came from the lower floors of the buildings nearby and from powerful police torches. He drew nearer the window, with Peel on the other side.

He saw a wall jutting out from this one, and a shadowy figure crouching on it. As he leaned farther out, he saw that it was the flat roof of an outhouse; there was a chimney stack. The man crouched by the stack with his right arm outstretched; and the gun was in his hand. The men below could see it much more clearly than Roger.

"Let's wait," Peel said. "We can get the okay for using guns on this; I can be back with a couple in twenty minutes. Or we could send—"

Roger said: "I don't want him to kill himself." He went farther forward, and knew that the man on the roof could see him. He couldn't see the other's face. He called: "Latimer, don't be a fool. Come back."

There was no reply.

Roger said: "You're only making it worse for yourself. We shan't ill-treat you. Come and talk it over."

"Keep away!" the man muttered.

"You can't do any good by using that gun—you won't help Meg or yourself."

Roger was now clearly outlined against the window, and could see that it was a simple matter of stepping out onto the roof. He was an easy target. He began to climb over the window sill.

"Don't be a fool!" hissed Peel. "He's mad; he'll shoot."

"You've told Meg and her sister that you haven't killed anyone," Roger said in a quiet, reassuring voice, "and if that's true, you haven't anything to worry about."

"It's true! But you'll frame me, you swine."

"You've got it all wrong, Latimer. We won't frame an innocent man. That's a promise."

Roger ducked beneath the top of the window, and then drew his other leg through. He stood on the roof, two or three yards from the man with the gun. Another powerful light flashed on below. It shone on the man by the chimney stack, giving a distorted view of his face, making his eyes look empty like those of a skeleton. Roger put one hand in his pocket, and moved a little nearer.

"Keep back!"

"I'm not going to keep back," said Roger. "I don't believe you're a fool, Latimer. You know if you shoot me, you'll be hanged. You won't be hanged if you didn't kill the others. So there's no point in shooting me, is there?"

He went still nearer. It was impossible to

be sure that the man was Latimer, but he didn't think there was any serious doubt now. Everyone else was silent; it was almost possible to hear the hush. Torches were kept steady, and he could see much more clearly; if it weren't for the shadow of the chimney stack, he would have been able to see all of the crouching man's face. Only four or five feet separated them now, and he could not only see the gun, but the shadow of it against the wall behind the chimney.

He drew his hand out of his pocket, with his cigarette case in it, took out a cigarette and lit it slowly—and then tossed the case. It struck against the man's arm. Roger leaped, and smashed a blow at the shadowy face. The man fell back, the gun dropped. Roger grabbed his outflung wrist, and pulled him forward. The man started to struggle— then squealed, as Roger pulled him round and forced his hand behind him in a hammer lock.

Peel was scrambling through the window.

"All over," Roger said. He was covered with cold sweat. "Is it Latimer?"

Peel could see the man clearly in the light.

"Of course it's Latimer," he said.

Latimer climbed through the window into the room, and stood shivering. The woman had been taken away. Latimer licked his lips and looked round. Peel climbed in, with the gun in his hand. A big C.I.D. man with stiff graying hair moved across and took Latimer's left wrist; handcuffs clicked.

"I didn't kill anyone!" gasped Latimer.

He wanted a shave, blue-black stubble made a shading on his chin and cheeks. There were dark patches under his eyes. He hadn't washed for some time and there was a streak of dirt across his forehead. His lips stayed parted, and he couldn't stop them from trembling; he was shivering from head to foot. His lower lip jutted out, and his short upper lip looked as if it had a mustache rubbed on with black crayon. His clothes were rumpled and dirty.

"I didn't kill anyone!"

"If you didn't, we'll prove it," said Roger, still calmly. "Let's have a look at his gun, Jim."

"It's a .32," Peel said.

The murders had been committed with an automatic of this size. It was squat, gray, ugly-looking. Roger sniffed it; there was nothing to suggest that it had been fired recently.

"I didn't shoot anyone!"

"You were going to shoot then," Peel said roughly.

"Easy." Roger unfastened the magazine, opening up the handle. He looked inside, conscious of the tense gaze of the others.

Latimer was gasping, as if he had been running.

"I didn't shoot anyone!"

"Well, you couldn't have shot me," said Roger. "It's empty. Did you know it was empty?"

"Of course I did. I—I only wanted to frighten you. I didn't kill anyone." Latimer drew in a deep, sobbing breath. "Give me—give me a drink."

Roger took out his flask and handed it to Peel. Latimer gulped the brandy down, then drew the back of his hand across his forehead; he was still trembling. Roger shut the gun and slipped it into his pocket. From outside, someone shouted to ask if everything were all right. Peel went to the window to reassure them.

Latimer said: "West, I didn't kill anyone. I was

202

dead scared. I thought you'd get me for selling that snow, and—I thought I was being framed. I was being proved guilty before I had a chance. I—I lost my nerve. I just lost my nerve, but I didn't kill anyone. I haven't done anyone any harm. That's the truth. All I wanted was to get out of the country; if I'd had enough money I could have fixed it. Meg—Meg brought me the money. Don't blame her, I made her."

"You nearly choked the life out of her."

Latimer opened his mouth. *"What?"*

"At Pullinger Street."

"I didn't touch her. I know I cracked that policeman's head, but I lost my nerve; all I could think about was getting away. He—he didn't die, did he?"

Roger didn't answer.

Latimer shrieked: "He couldn't have died; I didn't hit him hard enough. I haven't killed anyone; I've never had any ammunition for that gun. I couldn't have killed anyone."

Roger said flatly: "What about Raymond Arlen?"

"I didn't kill him!"

"Seen him lately?"

"No—yes. Yes, I saw him, once, only for a few minutes, a couple of days ago. He found me. But I didn't kill him—I didn't kill anyone." Latimer licked his lips, and his voice fell away. "I swear I didn't; but you'll hang me for it, I know you'll hang me."

"Let's get along to the Yard," said Roger.

Chatworth, burly and bustling like a farmer late for a sellers' market, thrust open the door of Roger's office. Roger had the telephone at his ear, waved and pointed to a chair. Chatworth muttered something, sat down and lit a cigarette.

"I'll come up," Roger said, and put down the receiver. "That was Ballistics; they're checking the gun—Scrymegour came in specially for the job. Like to come with me, sir?"

"Yes. Nice work, Roger."

"He couldn't dodge us all the time," Roger said. "It was fairly straightforward, after all. Margaret Sharp would sell her soul for him, and she worked with another woman—one of Latimer's snow customers. Latimer's done a lot of dope trafficking in a small way; the woman who drove the car up for Margaret Sharp did it because she was promised some shots if she would. We've picked her up; Peel's questioning her now. Margaret Sharp's flopped out."

"Told the press yet?"

Roger grinned. "I have!"

"There's someone else I want to tell," said Chatworth. "Let's get upstairs."

Scrymegour, who lived near the Yard, was with the night-duty man in the little Ballistics room. There was a faint smell of cordite; the automatic had been fired at a sheet of lead fastened on one wall. There were two bullets on the bench next to the special microscope, and two halves were beneath the lens, with Scrymegour peering at them. He didn't glance up, and Chatworth didn't interrupt him, although the duty man stiffened almost to attention.

Chatworth sniffed, and fiddled with one of the bullets.

"Can't fail," he said.

"What can't fail?" asked Scrymegour, straightening up. He turned, and started. "Good evening, sir!"

"Evening. Same gun?"

"No," said Scrymegour.

Roger looked and Chatworth looked; when the bullets were magnified and the markings showed up clearly, it was obvious that they didn't match. This wasn't the gun that had been used to kill the Arlens or Lionel Bennett. Chatworth looked ludicrously disappointed, Scrymegour sardonic. Roger picked up the bullet fired from Latimer's gun, and tossed it up, caught it, and said: "Let's find out if we've anything that does match up, Scrymmy."

"Can do. Tonight?"

"Please."

"Okay," said Scrymegour. "Sorry this one's a washout."

Chatworth said: "He probably had another gun," and then rubbed his bull-like neck and grinned ruefully. "What's going on in that mind of yours, West?" It was always "West" if anyone else was about.

"He could have put one across us," said Roger. "It would be a neat trick, to have this gun which hasn't been used for a while and certainly wasn't used to kill our trio, so that it looked as if part of his story was true. He just recites the same story— he didn't kill anyone. I wish there wasn't talk of a mystery man."

"Cheese it," said Scrymegour.

"We'll go to my office," said Chatworth. He led the way, deflated as a child disappointed of a new toy; but that mood wouldn't last long. He went straight to his desk and took out a bottle of whisky, a syphon and two glasses. "Have a drink," he said, and poured out, then squirted soda. "What do you make of it, Roger?"

"It's a bit early to say," said Roger. "We've got the man we wanted, and I think he'd have a job to prove his innocence; but we need to find that gun. The only helpful admission he made was that he saw Raymond Arlen a day or two ago, but he hasn't said anything else. He's closed up—he seems so frightened that he hasn't a cheep in him. Almost too frightened."

"Dope?" Chatworth asked.

"Could be."

Chatworth said: "Roger, I've been giving a lot of thought to this case—now then, don't grin at me. Deep thought. The dope angle hasn't cropped up much, but we knew Latimer was involved in it, didn't we? This woman Sharp—Margaret Sharp—hasn't behaved normally. Could she be an addict? If she is, and if Latimer is, they may have kept themselves going on the stuff and folded up when they couldn't get supplies."

"Oh, yes," said Roger. He looked thoughtfully at his whisky. "We've had Meg Sharp in a nursing home, and no doctor suggested recent drug addiction—only that she'd been doped that night. I agree, she behaves like a dopey. Pity about that gun—but we needn't tell the press about that."

Chatworth gave an explosive laugh.

"I'm waiting to see the morning papers," he said. "I oughtn't to give a damn what they say, but they certainly got under my skin. Anyhow, we've got him all right now; up to you to build up the case and make sure he hangs."

"Or goes to Broadmoor."

Chatworth frowned. "Meaning, he'll plead insanity."

"If his lawyers have any sense, he will—and they'll have plenty of sense. It'll be a chance of a lifetime to hit the headlines; there's going to be some fun before this case is over."

"If you go on like this, you'll be depressing me," said Chatworth. "Anything you want now?"

"No, thanks. I've arranged for Margaret Sharp to go back to the nursing home; she's no good for anything as she is. They'll tell us whether she's suffering from drugs or not—I shouldn't think she is. I'll go down and have another shot at Latimer, but if he's in the same mood, he'll be so shivery that I won't be able to get any sense out of him at all."

"I tell you I didn't kill anyone," sobbed Latimer. "I didn't kill anyone!"

There was no trace of the cigarette cases, money and other valuables stolen from the murdered men.

22

Big News

Roger winked at Janet, who lay in bed with her dark hair spread over the pillow and her eyes heavy with sleep. He got out of bed and went to the window. It was nearly half past seven—the time the paper boy usually arrived. There was no sign of him in the street. Roger put the kettle on the gas ring, yawned and stretched, and went out of the bedroom, leaving Janet snug and with her eyes closed. The boys were together in Scoopy's room, whispering. Roger looked in. They were sitting together in Scoopy's single bed, with a volume of the *Children's Encyclopedia* in front of them; they weren't able to read it, but the pictures fascinated them.

"This is a funny shell, Daddy," Scoopy announced seriously, and pointed. "It's got a lot of things sticking out of it. What is it?"

"Eh? Oh, just a seashell," said Roger, glancing at the colored plate. "Lovely, isn't it? What about saying good morning?"

"Morning," said Scoopy.

"Hallo," said Richard, meekly.

Roger rumpled their hair, and went out. The kettle was nearly boiling, and Janet was still pretending to be asleep. The front gate banged; paper boy! He hurried downstairs and pulled the papers out of the letter box, opened the *Echo* as he went back.

"Darling!" called Janet. "The kettle."

"Coming!"

He hurried upstairs, glimpsing the headlines.

WEST CATCHES LATIMER
DISARMS DANGEROUS GUNMAN

He glanced at another paper—the *Cry*—as he went into the bedroom. The kettle was boiling furiously, steaming the mirror over the mantelpiece.

LATIMER CAUGHT IN ROOF BATTLE
WEST MAKES ARREST

He dropped the newspapers and made the tea, yawned, picked up a paper and flung it across to Janet, who was now lying with her eyes wide open, but still sleepy. The boys were coming along the passage, unusually quiet for early morning.

"See what a sensational husband you have," said Roger.

Janet took the paper, glanced at it, and gasped: "Roger!"

"Hm-hm?"

"You didn't tell me you'd disarmed him."

"Anyone can take an empty gun off a chap."

"Empty!"

"Between you and me, it was empty. That's how heroes are made. For the next couple of days we

209

shall have the press telling us how right they were and how efficient the Yard is."

"I think it's a crime," said Janet. "In these days you ought to be armed all the time."

"And then you'd be jumping out of your skin in case the gun went off by accident while it was in my pocket," said Roger. He poured out tea. "What about saying good morning to Mummy, boys?"

"It's a *very* funny shell," said Scoopy.

"Morning, Mum," said Richard. "I'm thirsty." He toddled across for his orange juice, while Scoopy seized the nearest paper and opened it wide and shrieked! "*Look!*"

Richard drank, calmly.

"What?"

"It's Daddy—look!" Scoopy's eyes were bright, his cheeks glowed. "A picture of Daddy in the paper again—did you arrest a man last night, Daddy?"

"Yes, old chap, I'm afraid so."

"*I'm* going to be a policeman, too," announced Richard. "I'm going to be on traffic duty; that's a very important job."

"Silly," said Scoopy. "I'm going to be a detective. It's not a very *good* picture, Daddy, is it?"

"Good enough," said Roger.

"Can I cut it out and take it to school?" asked Scoopy.

"Tomorrow, maybe."

Roger lit a cigarette, and looked at the *Echo* again. It had the full story, with elaborations; he chuckled now and then. The other papers showed the same *volte face*. But after the first amused interest he became thoughtful; and remained thoughtful at the breakfast table and as he took the boys to school. But at the Yard he found Abbott just going in, smiling almost warmly. Eddie Day, the forgery expert, was grinning all over his face. There was an added briskness to the "good mornings"—the Yard was enjoying itself, and the measure of that proved the measure of its gloom until the previous night.

Sloan was in, with papers on his desk.

"Hallo, Roger! Nice work."

"Not so nice as it sounds."

"Oh, forget it," said Sloan. "It took a hell of a nerve to go out onto that roof. I think you're crazy; there wasn't any need to take a chance like that."

"We wanted to make sure he was alive," said Roger. "I had an idea that he might throw himself off the roof if we started threatening him with cannons. You know about the gun, I suppose."

"Yes. Pity. But it doesn't make much difference; you've enough to hang him."

"I'm not so sure," said Roger. "I think he ought to be hanged, but I've a nasty feeling that there's plenty of room for him to escape. How did you get on yesterday?"

"So-so. I'm seeing Lionel Bennett's lawyers this morning. I—"

The telephone bell rang.

"Hallo?" He held out the receiver. "A friend of yours," he said.

A throaty and somewhat nervous voice sounded at the other end of the line.

"Chief Inspector West?"

"Speaking."

"This is Mr. Bennett—Mr. Arthur Bennett. Is what I read in the papers this morning quite true?"

"Oh, we've caught Latimer," said Roger.

"Excellent, excellent," said Mr. Arthur Bennett. "I knew that it was only a matter of time, of course, but I confess I was nervous. Very nervous. Especially after the attack on my dear sister. I congratulate you, Chief Inspector; it was obviously a most courageous act on your part—most courageous. And I shall sleep much more easily—so will my brother. We're delighted—delighted."

"Good," said Roger, and wondered why the man had troubled to telephone.

"Of course I am worried about the situation," Bennett went on. "Most worried. The relationship is—er—bound to come out, I suppose?"

"I'm afraid so." Roger held his punches.

Bennett made a noise which sounded like *tck-tck*.

"Yes. Yes, I suppose so. On the other hand, it would only be necessary to—ah—to prove a motive, wouldn't it? If in fact Latimer has some other motive, or—and I really believe this is possible— if in fact he *isn't* Simon Arlen's son, then there would be no need for this hurtful matter to come into the open. Would there?"

"We'll have to prove identity," said Roger.

"You will, of course, of course." Bennett sounded more cheerful. "And if reasonable doubt could be shown—if for instance we could prove that Simon Arlen's son is alive somewhere else, or even that he is dead—that would constitute all the proof needed."

"Yes. But how can you do that?"

"We can *try*," breathed Bennett. "After all, think of the pain that such revelations will cause to so many people. My wife, my sister-in-law, my poor sister, and all the children, my nieces and nephews. It will be a dark and heavy shadow; it might have most grievous results. I feel bound to do everything I can to save them all from that, Chief Inspector, and I am sure I can rely upon your

212

discretion until—until such time as there is un-doubted proof of his identity."

"You can."

"Thank you, thank you," breathed Bennett. "I'm grateful. Good-by, Mr. West. I hope we meet again in somewhat happier circumstances; I do indeed. Good-by."

He hung up.

Roger put his receiver back and looked at it, scowling.

"What's he up to?" asked Sloan.

"I'm not sure," said Roger. "He's no fool, but he pretends to be one. Now he thinks he might be able to prove that the real son of Simon Arlen is someone else. He said he didn't know a thing about the son when I saw him, but he's now think-ing differently. I wonder why Latimer saw Ray-mond Arlen."

Sloan shrugged.

Roger said: "I'll go and see Latimer. Then after the hearing I think I'll slip up to Birmingham again. If you can get through with your job this morning, we'll go up together."

"Don't you think we've got the right man?"

"I'm as worried as hell," Roger growled.

Latimer said that he had telephoned Raymond Arlen before the murder train began; that he had discovered the relationship and had tried to per-suade Arlen to give him some money. Arlen had refused. He swore that he had not seen any of the others in the family, except Muriel Arlen. And he said that he had started to try to get in with his family, without any definite plans, had set out to meet Muriel Arlen and fallen in love with her.

He was much more self-possessed, more the man

213

whom Muriel Arlen knew; and he seemed confident that he would come through safely. Shaved, bathed, alert, he seemed to be a different man from the shivering creature on the roof. Looking at him, Roger felt cold dread: that the murderer was still at large.

Latimer was brought up at Bow Street, and the hearing started at a quarter to eleven. Roger made the charge—assault on the person of a police officer, Charles Smithson, who was proceeding in the course of his duty. Roger asked for an eight-day remand in custody, pending further inquiries. The formal charge and request took less than two minutes, and Roger stepped down from the box.

The magistrate, a middle-aged man with bushy eyebrows and small glasses, peered round the court.

"Is the accused represented in Court?"

The magistrate's clerk stood up and whispered; and another man stood up from the solicitors' benches. Roger had noticed him before—Llewellyn, a member of a leading firm of West End solicitors.

The magistrate peered at Llewellyn over the top of his glasses.

"Yes, Mr. Llewellyn?"

"I represent the accused, your worship, and ask for bail."

The reporters, lined up at benches behind him, made furious notes and whispered. The crowded public gallery sat back to relish this unexpected development.

"Bail, eh?" asked the magistrate. "Bail? No, I don't think so; this is a serious charge; I don't think so. No, Mr. Llewellyn. You may, of course, apply again at the next hearing. The case is adjourned for eight days."

Llewellyn made no secret of the fact that Mrs. Wilfred Arlen had engaged him to act for the man who might have killed her husband.

The press and the public didn't know it, but there might be more murders; Latimer might not be the killer. That possibility got under Roger's skin. He was on edge to get to Birmingham, but there was a message from Sloan at the Yard.

"Lionel Bennett's lawyer can tell us plenty—advise you don't leave for Birmingham until I've seen you."

Sloan wouldn't ask for delay unless he were sure that it mattered.

He rang up, just after three o'clock.

"Sorry I'm late, Roger, but it's worth it. I've talked to the Bennett family lawyer, a man named Pye. Simon Arlen was once a very rich man, but the son they farmed out didn't get a penny of his fortune. How about finding out if the Birmingham Bennetts can tell us what happened to it?"

"Get here as soon as you can, and let's hurry," Roger said.

23

Arthur Bennett Hurries

Ernest Bennett sat in his office in New Street, Birmingham. It was a small but well-appointed office, and in glass cases fastened to the walls were samples of the small tools which he and his brother made, through the firm of Bennett Brothers Limited, and which they had made for many years. The office was spick and span; Ernest was spick and span, but obviously agitated—so agitated that he bit at his nails as he stared at the telephone.

As if with sudden decision, he snatched it up.

"Get me Mr. Arthur."

"Yes, sir," said the operator.

Ernest waited, still biting his nails, but now looking out into the street. It was crowded, for it was early evening, and the offices and factories of the Midland metropolis were disgorging the workers.

After a long wait, Ernest snatched up the receiver again.

"I asked for Mr. Arthur!"

"I'm trying to find him, sir; they say he's still at the factory."

"Hurry," said Ernest, and banged down the receiver.

It rang, almost at once.

"Mr. Arthur, sir."

"Oh—Arthur. Arthur, listen. I have just had a most disturbing conversation with Pye....Of course you know Pye, Lionel's solicitor....Of course it isn't anything to worry about, but the police have been questioning him; they're making inquiries into Lionel's past. Eh?"

Arthur made a mumbling noise.

"I can't hear you properly," said Ernest testily. "I said the police have been making inquiries into Lionel's *past*. Pye is a pompous old fool; he said he thought that we should be informed, but I expect he told them everything they wanted to know. We'd better discuss the situation....Eh?"

He listened.

He squeaked: "Never mind social appointments!"

He listened again.

"Oh, very well; I'll come and see you. What time will you be home—seven? All right, I'll be there at seven-fifteen, and we shall have to have an hour alone, you understand....Mary's relatives can wait for a change. I'm sick of relations! Good-by."

He broke off, and began to bite his nails again. Then suddenly he stopped, threw out his chest, and said: "Nonsense! *I've* nothing to be afraid of." He lit a cigarette and smoked with an air of defiance, which was punctured when the telephone operator rang through to ask if she was wanted again. It was ten minutes past six.

"No, no! Go home. Go *home*." He replaced the receiver, stared at the windows in the buildings opposite, and added explosively: "Clock-watching

217

little brats—that's all the young people think about these days. Drat them!"

He stood up, and hurried out of the office, glaring at the girl who was already on her way, and went to his club. He was not in a social mood, but had two stiff whiskies before he left, a little after half past six. He had plenty of time to get to his brother's home, which was near Solihull, some distance from his own home. Then he ran into a stream of lorries and heavy traffic, and was forced to lose five minutes because of a minor breakdown with a bus. He fussed and stormed, and then crawled past the obstruction; but the stream of traffic took some time to thin out, and he was soon glancing at his watch and telling himself that he must hurry.

He had a Humber limousine, a car of which he was as proud as Lionel had been of his Rolls Royce. It had a fine burst of speed, and he did not pay much attention to the speed limit that night. On the outskirts of the city he turned into a side road, and was soon driving along country lanes. He had made a point of keeping off country roads for the past day or two. Now he was going too fast for safety on the twisting, turning road, but was a skillful driver and without nerves. Mastery of the car turned him into a different man.

He swung round a corner into a private road leading to Arthur's drive—about half a mile away.

It was getting dusk.

A figure jumped from the side of the road, and stood with hands raised.

He jammed on his brakes, but was going too fast to stop, swerved to avoid the still figure on the road, hit the bank, and nearly turned the car over. It stopped a few inches from the big, dark-clad fig-

ure with a trilby hat, pulled low, a long mackin-
tosh which almost hid the trousers.

He screamed: "What on earth are you doing, you
fool?"

There was no answer, but the menacing figure
came slowly toward him—with an automatic in
his hand.

Bennett screamed again, but it was a different
sound. His mouth was wide open, terror screeched
—and the screech merged with the roar of the shot
and the flash of flame.

It was nearly four o'clock when Roger and Sloan
left London. They would be in Birmingham by
seven, perhaps a little before. Roger could see that
Sloan was jubilant, but didn't prompt him. Sloan
sat back, relaxing, smoking a cigarette, obviously
framing his words. When Sloan was as careful as
that, he had plenty on his mind.

"It's a new angle, all right, Roger," he said.

"Simon's money?"

"Piles of it. He was a millionaire."

"Well, well!"

"The family was wealthy before he inherited,
and he had the little something which turns
money into more money."

"I see."

"No doubt where he died," said Sloan. "He was
put away on a certificate issued by the Bennett
and Arlen family doctors. I've checked; the Bennetts' doctor is still alive. It was fairly easy to put
people away in those days, wasn't it?"

"So they say."

"Oh, it was easy. Anyhow, that was the only authority. Before he went inside Millionaire Simon
gave Lionel Bennett power of attorney—complete

power. If that wasn't enough, his wife did the same, and his wife signed the papers which enabled Lionel and the other Bennetts to farm the son out. Then the wife died. The money was equally divided among the surviving Bennetts—six families, in all. Simon's son was washed out, as far as money was concerned. If Simon Arlen hadn't been put away, the others wouldn't have started off with nearly a quarter of a million pounds apiece. There were lower death duties in those days; they did very nicely. Raymond and Wilfred Arlen were the youngest, of course—both at school. The Bennett brothers handled the whole thing, as the older generation of Arlens had died out. Wilfred and Raymond had no part in it—except taking the money. Raymond put a lot of his in a business, which went broke; the others were wiser—or luckier. What do you make of it?"

"I'd like to see Wilfred's and Raymond's wills—and Lionel Bennett's, for that matter."

Sloan gave a smug grin.

"I've seen 'em. We ought to have gone to them straight away. There's an identical clause in each. Two-thirds of the estate to wife and family, one-third to be shared equally among all surviving Arlens and Bennetts of the same generation. The two live Bennetts and Mrs. Drew get a tidy sum from Wilfred and Lionel, nothing to speak of from Raymond."

"There's an obvious possibility that Simon was actually put away so that the others could get hold of his money," Roger said. "Probably he was queer, had spells, actually used violence with his wife. The Bennetts, Lionel being the chief organizer, saw a wonderful chance and took it. But it might not have happened that way."

"If it did—"

"It would give Latimer, the son of Simon Arlen, a pretty good motive for hate."

"But who would have told him about it?"

"That's the big question."

Sloan said: "Meaning what?"

"Margaret Sharp says he 'found out.' How? He wouldn't be likely to remember the days of his infancy, would he? He was brought up as a Latimer. He didn't know the truth when he lived at home with his foster parents and Margaret, apparently —remember she said that they lost each other for some years. If she wasn't lying pretty slickly, he discovered the truth after his parents were dead. So—who told him, and why?"

"Someone else with a reason for hate?"

Roger said dreamily: "It could be, couldn't it? Let's go a step farther than we have. Let's imagine that one of the family was hard up. Raymond, for instance, as he lost his capital. Let's imagine that he told Latimer and egged Latimer on, believing that there was a chance that Latimer also had homicidal tendencies. They would show. Let's imagine that the share clause in each will was a kind of gentleman's agreement. And let's suppose that the murder motive was to persuade Latimer to kill off the family, so that a useful pile came to Raymond—or whoever gave Latimer the information. Murder by proxy, as it were."

"And then Latimer turned on Raymond?"

"Could be," said Roger.

"What do you expect to get out of the Bennetts?"

"They may know more than they've told us. They're pretty jittery already, about this shameful thing in their past, and it'll be more shameful if it's suggested that in fact Simon wasn't insane, and that it was a plot to get hold of his money. With

221

that hanging over their heads, they'll tell everything they can, I fancy."

Sloan smiled. "I like seeing you at work! Who are you going to see first?"

"Arthur," said Roger. "He's the younger, and he seems to have a decent streak. We might get everything out of him with a lot less trouble than we got it out of Ernest. Velvet glove with Arthur, and if necessary—"

"Iron mitt for Ernest!"

The traffic slackened, and Sloan stepped on the accelerator.

Arthur Bennett's house was much older than Ernest's—a big, red brick place with tall, narrow windows. It stood in an acre or more of ground at the end of the long private road, and the garden was in perfect order; they could see that as they went along the drive, just after seven o'clock. It was hardly dusk; the brightness of the day was only just beginning to fade, and the colors in the flowers in the beds beneath the windows and on either side of the drive showed in all their beauty. At one side of the house were rose gardens and terraces, giving promise of beauty in June.

There was a big sweep in the drive in front of the house. Sloan stopped opposite the front door, and they looked at the big, brown-painted door and the brightly polished brass bell and knocker. No one stirred, but the birds were noisy; somewhere nearby a woodpecker was calling.

The door was opened by a middle-aged man, dressed in black; somehow, Roger hadn't expected Arthur to have a butler. The man was tall, with iron-gray hair, portly and stately; he spoke in a refined, muted voice, led them into the hall and then to a small room, switched on the light, promised them that he would not keep them waiting, and went off.

"Arthur will have time to get used to the idea," said Sloan.

"He won't keep us waiting."

Arthur didn't. He came in himself, bustling, hand in front of his mouth; but his lisping had gone; he had conquered the disability.

"Why, Mr. West, how are you?" He shook hands warmly with them both. "How are *you?* Most unexpected, but most fortuitous; I am expecting my brother any minute now. Most fortuitous. But come into the drawing room; you must have a drink—detectives *do* drink while on duty, I hope."

"Occasionally," said Roger. "Thanks very much."

"Come along, come along." Arthur led them across the big hall, with its huge oil paintings and massive doors, into a room which seemed to reek of the Victorian age. There was big furniture, an old grand piano, there were antimacassars on the chair backs, the rich Persian carpet looked old, but was in good condition. Lights sparkled from a chandelier onto glasses and bottles in a mahogany cabinet. "I think I can offer practically everything, practically everything," said Arthur, when he picked up a bottle; his hand wasn't quite steady. "Whisky?"

"Thank you."

Whisky bubbled, soda spurted.

"Your *very* good health," said Arthur. "I can't tell you how relieved I am at the news that Latimer is apprehended. It was alarming—we tried to make light of it the other day, but it *was* alarming. Latimer—"

"You knew Latimer was your cousin, didn't you?"

"Cousin! Well—yes, yes. That's how it looks, and it's a distressing thing to have to contemplate, Mr. West. My brother isn't sure, you know; he is always rather obstinate." Arthur gave a little laugh. "If he doesn't want a thing to be true, he will spend a fortune trying to prove that it isn't. He's like that. *Very* like that. I wonder why he hasn't arrived? He's due at seven fifteen, and he's a most punctual man. Most."

"It's only seven twenty," said Roger.

"Yes, we must allow him a little grace, mustn't we? And traffic is so thick in Birmingham; it really is getting a serious problem. Well—congratulations again, Mr. West, and I'm yours to command. Command," he repeated, and sipped his whisky.

"You're very good. Mr. Bennett, was there any shadow of doubt, at the time, about the mental condition of Simon Arlen?"

Arthur nearly dropped his glass.

"Doubt?"

Roger said: "It's a peculiar story. Your family doctor and your brother Lionel made the necessary application for Simon to be put away. We have to go deeply into the whole matter, of course."

"Why?" whispered Arthur. "What good—"

"We have to establish a motive for the murders, you know that. If Latimer believed that he had been cheated of his father's fortune, then it would explain many things, wouldn't it?"

Arthur said: "Oh, no. No!"

"The matter was handled by your elder brothers," said Roger. "Had you any doubts about it? Any uneasiness?"

Arthur didn't speak.

"Sufficient uneasiness to try to trace your cousin and to make some amends?" went on Roger. "That would reflect very great credit on you, Mr. Bennett, and in court—"

"*Court*," sighed Arthur. "You really think—" He broke off, and closed his eyes. He was holding his glass so awkwardly that whisky dripped onto the carpet. "It has really—really come to this. Well, well. Evil—evil will out. Mr. West, I—I have been unhappy about this for many years. *Many* years."

Roger said: "Why?"

"It was—a strange business, very strange. I knew Simon Arlen well. He was a strong-tempered, strong-willed man. I can remember that he gave Lionel and Ernest a thrashing, took on the two of them together, and—yes, he was wild, very angry indeed. He always flew into a rage when he was crossed, and yet—yet when he was certified it was a great shock to me. I'd rather—liked Simon. We got on better than the others, you see, and he was a fine, handsome man. I was always something of a weakling. I was out of England at the time; I came hurrying back. It was all over by then, and his poor wife was dead. And—I was suddenly a wealthy man. It wasn't until later that I began to wonder. Conscience—you know. But I was doing very well. I mentioned it to Lionel and Ernest, but they were most emphatic, and I took the line of least resistance. We—we came to an understanding."

He paused.

"About what?"

"Well, we were once *very* close together, so were the Arlens; we tried to insure against one having

225

bad fortune—left a portion of our estates to be shared. Yes."

He stopped.

"I know," said Roger.

"Oh." Arthur looked crestfallen. "You see the evidence of great family loyalty. Don't you? But—but occasionally, usually on the anniversary of Simon's birthday, I found all the old doubts rising. Some time ago; but I told you—I distinctly remember that I told you—I tried to trace his son. I failed. If only I had succeeded, this terrible thing might have been avoided. *The evil that men do,*" he added, with a whisper, and then straightened up. "But—I *may* be wrong. I may have been nursing false suspicions all these years."

Roger didn't speak.

Arthur said in an unsteady voice: "I don't know, I can only hope that I am wrong. I have been quite frank with you, Mr. West; you appreciate that—perhaps too frank. Ernest was here all the time; he knows much more about it than I do. Why—he's nearly a quarter of an hour late! It's *most* unlike him."

Roger said: "Where was he coming from?"

"The city. Birmingham—our office there. It's more convenient than at the factory. What *has* delayed him? It's most unlike him." He went across to the window and pulled one of the curtains aside. "No, there's no sign of the car, and it isn't all that dark. He needn't be so late as this." He turned away, but didn't put the curtain back into place. He stood against it, and his hand went to the back of his head, much as Georgina's had done when she was giving her signal. "I confess that I have been very jumpy at this hour of the evening for the past few days, very jumpy. But he's caught; there can't

226

be any danger now, can there? Can there? It was Latimer, it was—"

Roger watched him, and saw a movement just outside the window. He shouted, swift as thought, and moved. Arthur jumped. Roger thrust him aside and flung himself down, and a bullet smashed through the window.

24

Killer

Sloan turned and raced out of the room, thudding toward the front door, pulling it open and rushing into the garden. Roger saw the figure outside move, as he rolled over. Arthur had fallen and was trying to get up.

"Keep down!" snapped Roger.

Arthur flopped onto his stomach.

There was a flash and a roar, and more tinkling of glass. Then footsteps—Sloan's, as he rushed to the front of the house. As he got unsteadily to his feet, Roger saw the figure at the window turn and run. He flung the window up, as Sloan rushed past, into the semi-darkness. The assailant was thirty yards in front of Sloan, and running awkwardly; as if drunk.

Roger's knee pained him, slowing him down.

Sloan wasn't far behind the fleeing figure, which stopped and turned round. Roger shouted involuntarily: *"Down!"* Sloan saw the move, and flung himself to one side, and lost his balance. Shot and flash came simultaneously, but the gunman lost no time, raced for the side of the drive, trampled over the flower beds and made for the woods which lined the drive. Forcing himself to go faster, Roger passed Sloan.

"Careful!" Sloan cried.

He didn't follow; so he'd hurt himself.

Roger thought: "Not this time, you won't get away this time." Damn his knee. The trees were thick, and it was not so easy to see the assailant, who was now near the low wall which separated the garden from the trees. Roger expected to see him vault the wall; he didn't, but slowed down, turned again and fired.

The bullet went wide.

Roger ran to one side, was now against thick bushes, and couldn't be seen so easily. The light beyond was better, and he saw the shadowy form start to climb the wall, awkwardly. Roger went forward like a stone from a catapult. Another bullet came, but that also missed. Then he flung himself forward, grabbed a leg and heaved upward. The assailant toppled over the wall, and cried out. Roger hit against the wall, steadied, and put his hand on the top and hauled himself up. He could see the gunman below him, groping for something on the ground; groping for the gun. Roger jumped and flung himself bodily onto the gunman, jabbed at the nose, and then felt as if he were cushioned against feather pillows.

This wasn't a man; it was a woman.

Margaret Sharp didn't say a word. She wasn't badly hurt, just bruised and grazed. She stared at Roger blankly, with dull eyes, as if madness had been drained out of them.

*   *   *

It was nearly six o'clock next morning when Roger reached Middleton Street. Peel was already outside Number 122, Roger had telephoned him from Birmingham to be there. All he told Peel was that Margaret Sharp was being held on a charge of shooting with intent to murder, and he kept back the news that Ernest Bennett's body had been found in the car among the trees bordering the private road. Roger's eyes felt prickly from lack of sleep; he'd dozed in the car from Birmingham while Sloan had driven. Margaret was already in London.

Roger rang the bell under which was the card with Gina's and Meg's names. He rang again after a lapse of a few seconds, and listened intently; rang for a third time. Then they heard a sound instead, as of someone scuffling.

Georgina opened the door.

She was wearing a dark-blue dressing gown, heel-less slippers and a hair net. She looked sleepy and young, but at sight of them became startled and alarmed. She stood aside, without speaking; and she stared at Peel, not Roger.

"Sorry to worry you so early," Roger said. "May we go upstairs?"

He led the way.

"What's—happened?"

Roger didn't answer, Peel returned a blank gaze to Georgina's questioning eyes. She caught her breath, and started after Roger.

"It's Meg. Meg's not—dead?"

"No," Roger said over his shoulder.

Georgina didn't speak again until they were in the big living room. It was well past dawn, but there was a cold gray light. The room was tidy, but

230

looked forlorn, almost unused. Georgina wrapped the dressing gown more tightly about her, and stood with her back to the window.

"Don't torture me," she begged. "What's happened?"

"Why didn't you tell us that you knew your sister had killed these people?" asked Roger abruptly.

"*Meg*? Killed someone?" The words were like a long sigh. "Don't be ridiculous."

But there was no spirit in her voice; she was frightened.

"You knew, didn't you?"

"Of course I didn't know anything of the kind. I don't believe it's true. Latimer—but you caught him! You caught him. Jim!" She swung round on Peel. "You came yesterday afternoon and told me he was caught, and that Meg was in a nursing home; you said there was nothing to worry about. Did you lie to me? Jim!"

She clutched his hand.

Roger said: "He hasn't lied. Everything he told you was true. But now we know the murderer was your sister. She must have had the gun here."

"I've never seen a gun!"

"She must have been away at the time of each murder, and you must have known it. Why not tell us the truth, Miss Sharp? You suspected it all along; that's why you went to see Latimer. You knew that he'd planned it, she did it. That's why you went to him with the money; he threatened to tell us the truth if you didn't. Lying won't help now."

"Oh, it isn't true." She caught her breath, and her eyes looked enormous. "It can't be true, not Meg—*Meg* wouldn't kill. He—he's tried to blame her. That must be it."

Roger said: "Miss Sharp, we've had plenty of these bright ideas from your sister and from you. We've watched the way you've both behaved, and there's been no reason in it. You said yourself that your sister wasn't behaving normally; you forgot to add that you weren't. You aren't necessarily involved. It's not an indictable offense to withhold information from the police. Certainly it would be hard to blame you, if all you've done is try to shield your sister. We'll find out if there's anything else, so let's have all the truth now."

She didn't move—just stared at him.

"Oh, but it's not true. I didn't suspect it, I didn't dream—I don't believe it now. Not Meg. Latimer's fooled you, and—"

"You knew they were related—she was his foster sister. Didn't you?"

"I know you suggested they were related," said Georgina. She moved toward Peel. They must have made a lot of progress the previous afternoon, for she took his hand. "Jim, don't let him talk like this. He may believe it, but you can't—not that I did anything like that. And Jim—is it true? Was it Meg?"

Peel nodded.

She said: "Oh, Meg, *why?*"

She turned away, and fumbled for a cigarette from a box on a low table. She put it to her lips. Peel began to take out his lighter, but Roger shook his head, and Georgina took a box of matches and struck one; it broke off, and the flaming head hit the carpet. Peel trod it out. She didn't strike another, just stood there with the unlit cigarette in her mouth.

Then: "She didn't kill them," she said slowly. "I *know* she didn't. She was here all that first eve-

232

ning, when Wilfred Arlen was killed. Every minute of it."

"We've only your word for that."

"No, you haven't," said Georgina, and there was a glint in her eyes; she was bracing herself against the shock, seeking grounds for hope. "We had visitors—two people from the flat below; they stayed for half an hour. Meg didn't kill Wilfred Arlen, and —she was here when one of the others was killed. When you were at York. What is all this?" She looked younger, and her eyes were bright with suspicion. "What are you trying to do?"

"Sorry," said Roger briefly. "She is being held on a charge of murder, Miss Sharp. We know beyond all reasonable doubt that she killed Mr. Ernest Bennett last night. She ran away from the nursing home. She used the gun which was used to kill the others. You've made the other alibi for her."

"Oh, no," said Georgina; but the brightness had gone. "Another? Last night? And—"

"And Latimer was in jail, so it wasn't him."

Georgina fumbled for the matches again, lit one successfully, and drew in the smoke. She coughed.

"I don't know about last night. It doesn't seem reasonable—not Meg, to kill. But she certainly didn't kill Wilfred Arlen; that's quite impossible. If she didn't—who did? Latimer?"

"Did you see anyone except Latimer at the house near Praed Street?"

"No."

"Your sister said that someone else was there. Have you any idea who it was?"

"No."

"Do you know any other friends, who might be involved?"

"No."

"Did you ever meet Raymond Arlen?"

She shook her head, and this time just whispered: "No."

"Did your sister know him?"

"I don't know," she said. "I don't think so; I never heard her mention him." She drew in smoke again, and moved to Peel, who was standing awkwardly at ease. "Jim, is this all true? I can't believe him, but I don't think you would lie to me. Is Meg under arrest?"

"Yes, Gina."

"I—see." She backed away, and sank into a chair as if the strength had drained out of her. "And you can prove it; she's going to be hanged. Poor, poor Meg! I knew it wasn't right; there was something evil in it—there was evil in Latimer, and she couldn't see it. She was quite blind, and I think she loved him. He turned her bad." Georgina didn't close her eyes, but did not appear to notice either of the men. "I sensed it, from the beginning. She started to take drugs, and he gave them to her; but I fought against that, and she stopped. At least, I thought she stopped; she seemed to get better. But she turned vengeful because of it, she began to hate me. How did he do it? How did he manage to turn *her* bad?"

She stopped, and darted a glance at Roger.

"I must see her. I must, do you understand? Take me to her."

At the Yard, Sloan said: "She's right, of course she's right—Meg couldn't have killed the others."

"We hardly needed telling that," said Roger.

"And we haven't found the stolen goods yet." Roger didn't answer.

234

25

The Lovers

Margaret looked up from the single bed in the cell at Cannon Row, and nodded distantly to Georgina. She showed no hostility and no real interest, and she hardly spoke a word. Roger, who was by the door of the cell with the station sergeant, gave them ten minutes, then went in and put a hand on Georgina's arm.

"Better come away now."

Georgina turned, and there was a film of tears in her eyes. She looked back at her sister, but Meg was staring at the ceiling as if she were completely disinterested in anything and anyone. She had hardly spoken since she had been charged.

In the courtyard, walking toward the Yard itself, Georgina said in a steady voice: "I'll spend every penny I have to help her. You know that, don't you? I still can't believe it; that man must have the Devil in him."

"How long has she been jealous of you?"

"Jealous?"

"How long has she resented the fact that you

have a steady job, of its kind, and earn fairly good money?"

"She's never really been happy about that, I suppose. But we've shared everything; that was the understanding we had as we started to live together. Meg had some money of her own—not much, but more than I. We lived very modestly until I started to earn, and I owed her a lot and didn't mind paying it back. I wanted her to be—happy. Mr. West, is there anything you can do to help her?"

Roger said: "I'm a policeman and have a policeman's job, Miss Sharp. So has Jim Peel. Don't forget that, will you?"

She walked on, and stumbled at the first of the flight of stone steps.

Sloan came bustling into the office, scowling. He flung his hat on a chair and wrenched at his tie until the ends hung down. He lit a cigarette.

"Well, where do we go from here? How the hell did Meg get out?"

"She slipped away after tea—they have it at the nursing home at half past three. No one went in to her until after six. Simple."

"Damnable! We still want our mystery man. And what about Latimer? This lets him out—we wouldn't have a chance in hell of making the case stick, as Meg Sharp had the gun. Don't you agree?"

"Things have brightened for Latimer," Roger agreed.

"And darkened for us. Roger, what the devil is behind all this?"

Roger smiled faintly. "Something simple, I think. Hate plus greed."

"Equals murder this time—but—by whom?"

Roger said: "Don't go too fast. What do we know? That the son of Simon Arlen was undoubtedly cheated, robbed of his birthright; and when that's over a million pounds, it's a pretty useful birthright. Small wonder Simon's son thought that he had a right to get some back."

"But Latimer—"

"And how would he get any?" asked Roger, absently. "By killing and robbing the victims of a few thousand pounds' worth of jewels? That might make him happy, but it wouldn't last him for long, and I think he was after big money. How would he get it?"

"You're asking," Sloan said.

"He *might* get his hands on it if part of the fortune fell into the hands of one of the relatives," said Roger. "Remember those wills. On the death of any of the family, a large sum went to the survivors. At the moment there are two left. Those two share a pretty big fortune between them, don't they?"

"Arthur Bennett and Mrs. Drew?"

"Wait a minute," Roger said. "Remember those wills. Remember that with every death in the family the survivors became better off. That means that Arthur Bennett has recently come into large chunks of the family fortune."

"Where would he come into the crimes?" demanded Sloan.

"Supposing he had made an arrangement with Arnold, the dispossessed son of Simon," Roger said, very deliberately. "Supposing Arthur Bennett has connived at these murders—and will share his profits with his nephew. How would it look then?"

"My God!" ejaculated Sloan.

"So if we were to find out that the business of

Bennett Brothers isn't financially sound, and that Arthur is in need of money, it would give him the necessary motive," Roger went on mildly.

"I'll be living in Birmingham, soon," Sloan said. "What a mind you've got!"

Margaret Sharp stood in the dock, pale-faced and dry-eyed, and didn't speak. The charge was over briefly, and she was remanded in custody for eight days. Georgina was in the public gallery.

Roger spent the rest of the day making a round of the families, except Arthur Bennett and Mrs. Drew. Mrs. Muriel Arlen was aloof, Dennis wasn't at home. Mrs. Raymond Arlen was still badly shocked, and her own mother was with her. Mrs. Lionel Bennett was with relatives who lived nearby. Not one of them could recall any suggestion that the Bennett Brothers had asked for loans or given any hint that they were in financial trouble. That part of it was an empty day.

Other things filled it.

There was no shadow of doubt that Margaret Sharp had not killed anyone, until she had shot Ernest. She had an indisputable alibi for each of the other crimes. Latimer continued to swear that he knew nothing about it, but was now less abject. There were no reports of any close friend of Margaret's who might have killed the others; no further hint of a mystery man.

Roger was back at the Yard soon after five o'clock, and found a message that Peel would like to see him. He rang for the sergeant.

"Come in, Jim—how are things?"

"I'm all right," Peel said. "You can guess what I feel, but I can't do anything about that. Roger, tell me straight—do you think Georgina is involved?"

"No."

Peel said quickly: "Is that on the level?"

"Flat as it can be, Jim. Forget it. It looks as if you'll find Georgina about as forlorn and miserable as a woman can be, and you don't have to be on duty all the time."

"It's a load off my mind," said Peel. "I've been telling myself you thought she was in it. What about this man who's supposed to have been at Pullinger Street?"

"There wasn't any man. Latimer and Meg did the jobs between them," Roger said. "We haven't any proof yet, but I'm pretty sure that Latimer committed the early crimes, and kept doubling on his tracks. He showed up in different places as different types of men. Thus he had some money, but hounded the Sharps and others for more, to make him look broke. If he were ever caught, he hoped that the trial would be hopelessly confused—that his two guises would make it seem very unlikely that he'd robbed anyone."

Peel said: "I'm beginning to see."

"He had another trick planned, because he knew he could rely on Margaret's love and self-sacrifice. If he were arrested and charged with the murders, Margaret was to kill another member of the family in exactly the same way as the others had been killed. This would make it look almost certain that the real killer was still at liberty, and we'd got the wrong man. Latimer must have believed that there was a good chance that this would come off, and that he and Margaret might set up home together. The plot failed because Margaret didn't do her part of the job well enough."

"Is this—certain?"

"Not yet," said Roger. "The stickiest part will be

239

getting proof, but we've a line."

He looked up as footsteps sounded in the passage outside, and grinned when Sloan positively stormed in. Sloan carried a large envelope and slapped it down on the desk.

"Any luck?" asked Roger mildly.

"Luck! Bennett Brothers Limited are down the drain. They've been fighting against bankruptcy for years. Every stick and stone they possessed was mortgaged."

"Not bad," said Roger. "It's a pity it's so far to Birmingham."

"No need to go to Birmingham," Sloan said triumphantly. "I've brought Arthur along with me. He came like a lamb. I can't imagine why, but he seemed overjoyed when I said that Latimer was dangerously ill and hinted that he'd almost certainly die. He's *very* sorry for poor Simon's son."

Roger's smile stopped at his eyes.

"Most unprofessional," he said. "Still, as toothless Arthur's here, we may as well have a chat with him. Or better still—" He broke off, and stretched for the telephone. "Where is he?"

"In the waiting room."

"Hallo," said Roger into the telephone. "Brixton Jail, in a hurry." He held on until the remand prison was on the other end of the line. "West here. . . . Yes, it's about Latimer. I'm going to send over for him; I want another little chat. How is he?"

"Well, how is he?" asked Sloan, when Roger replaced the receiver.

"Getting bolder and bolder," said Roger, "and talking about blackouts and he can't always remember what he's been doing—warming up nicely for the insanity plea. He's about as insane as our little Arthur."

"Going to put them face to face?" asked Peel.

"That's it—in the second waiting room. After all, they won't know that we're looking through a window, will they? We should know if they're buddies as soon as they set eyes on each other." He grinned. "I think we've reached the end now."

Arthur Bennett, wearing striped gray trousers and black coat, was sitting on an upright chair in one of the waiting rooms which had a communicating door with another. He jumped up as Roger entered, held out his hand and wrung Roger's fervently. He was eager and apparently cheerful, but that covered his nerves. His gums showed.

"I've been wanting to see you again, Chief Inspector. I haven't properly thanked you for the wonderful way in which you saved my life. Wonderful. Such courage! I'm desolated, of course. Poor Ernest! But—let us face it, life is sweet, and time will heal all wounds. Won't it?"

"Sooner or later," said Roger.

"Yes, yes. Time is a wonderful healer. I only wish they had tried *time* for poor Simon; but there it is, there it is. I hear that the man—Latimer—is sick."

"It's surprising how news spreads," said Roger blandly. "Is there anything new to tell me?"

"Oh, no. No, I don't think so. Doubtless as time goes on I shall remember details which you may find important, but—well, I confess I shall be very happy if poor Simon's boy dies. That may seem cruel, but in fact it would save such a lot of distress. Wouldn't it? No trial, no washing of dirty

241

linen—nothing. Nothing like that."

"We'd still have to deal with the woman Sharp."

"The woman—ah, yes. Yes. Tell me," asked Arthur, peering up short-sightedly, "has she confessed? Has she told you everything she knows?"

"I don't think she knows a great deal. She was in love with Simon's boy, and worked to try to save him."

"Really," breathed Arthur. "You know, Chief Inspector, it is remarkable how clever these people with unbalanced minds are, isn't it? Who else would have thought of a simple and yet crafty trick like Arnold and this woman? It isn't really surprising, I suppose, and yet—but how nearly it succeeded. The truth is, you know," he went on earnestly, "few people realize how capable the police are. You and all your colleagues in this wonderful establishment. They underestimate you, Chief Inspector."

"We usually catch up," said Roger.

A buzzer sounded; the signal that Latimer was now in the next room. The door opened and Sloan and Peel came in. Roger went across to the communicating door.

"I wonder if you'll come into this room, Mr. Bennett."

Roger thrust open the door.

Sloan and Peel went to a window, through which they could see into the next room, although no one in that room could see into this. Arthur went through cheerfully, peering about him short-sightedly. Roger let the door close, and nipped back to the window which looked like frosted glass from inside the room.

Latimer was sitting in a chair in a corner, and stood up abruptly as Arthur entered. Arthur caught sight of and recognized him. The two stared at each other, Arthur open-mouthed, Latimer with his hands clenched. He looked round swiftly, saw no one else, and said: "What the hell are you doing here?"

"Arnold!"

"So they've got you too," said Latimer, and began to laugh. "They've got you, you cunning old hypocrite. I thought you were going to get away with it. You ruddy fool, why did you let them catch you?"

26

Full Story

Roger slipped into the inner room.

Neither of the others saw him at first, they were too busy looking at each other. Arthur Bennett stood limp, body sagging, mouth wide open. Latimer relaxed, and the grin slowly faded from his face.

"They said—you were *ill*," sighed Arthur.

"Sure, I'm ill; *I'm* all right. I'm not sane, see. A few years at Broadmoor, and I'll be all right. But they won't be so kind to you, will they? They'll hang *you*."

"Arnold, don't," said Arthur faintly.

"Don't Arnold me," said Latimer. "We've messed it up. When they caught Margaret it put paid to any hope I had of being found not guilty; but remember—*I'm* crazy. But I have periods of sanity when my memory's good; that'll be a help."

"You—wouldn't—"

Latimer glanced round and saw Roger. He licked his lips, and backed away from Arthur Bennett, as if from something of which he was terribly afraid. Arthur sagged.

"So you're old friends," Roger murmured.

"Friends!" cried Latimer. "He put me up to it, he—" He broke off and licked his lips, his eyes became glazed, then stared wildly. He began to shiver. "I—I'm not well, I'm not well!" he gasped.

"We'll look after you," said Roger. "And I think it's time we had another little talk, Mr. Bennett."

Arthur mumbled, and his knees wobbled. Peel and Sloan came in, to look after Latimer, who was still putting on his act. Arthur allowed himself to be led out of the room, then collapsed onto a chair. It was ten minutes before he was able to start talking; but once he started, he wouldn't stop.

It was all Arnold's idea—

All Arnold's, that was, and Ernest's. His brother was really guilty.

He, Arthur, hadn't *wanted* any part in it....Yes, he and Ernest had arranged the identical clauses in the wills; they were not too sound financially, it seemed "only fair." Lionel and the Arlens hadn't argued much, the family skeleton had to be kept hidden. It was a conspirators' agreement.

Chatworth looked up from his desk, scowled, waved to a chair and then to cigarettes, and went on with the reports he was reading. Roger sat back, at ease, smoking, watching the shiny bald patch in the midst of Chatworth's grizzled forest of hair.

It was two hours since Latimer, or Arnold Arlen, and Arthur Bennett had been confronted with each other.

Chatworth pushed the papers aside and leaned back.

"Well, what's your latest version?"

"The final one, I think," said Roger. "Arthur and

Latimer have both talked; they couldn't blame each other fast enough once we really started on them. Arthur cracked first, and after that Latimer knew the game was up."

"How did it start?"

"Several years ago, when Latimer discovered who he was. It started in a queer way—he saw Raymond Arlen in a tube train, and the likeness was quite striking. So he wondered if he could get to know Raymond, and do himself a bit of good. He followed him, found out who he was, and when he went to see Raymond, it gave the man such a shock that Latimer knew there was a story behind it, and probed deep. He discovered the truth and suspected that he had been jockeyed out of a fortune, so he started to touch them all. He went round to each of the relatives in turn, and managed to get a little hush money—they called it a gift. Latimer then knew he was onto a good thing.

"In the course of it, he met Muriel Arlen. He says that he fell in love with her. I wouldn't know— she's certainly in love with him.

"Then he was approached by Arthur Bennett— not poor Ernest, but Arthur. Arthur was keeping up a good front, but had run through a fortune, and the business wasn't sound. He'd fixed the accounts, and he knew that the day of reckoning wasn't far off. And there was the glittering prize which would fall into the lap of the last surviving relation of Simon Arlen's generation.

"Latimer approached him for more money.

"Each says the other suggested the plot, and I wouldn't like to say who did. But it worked up nicely. Latimer knew he might be put away in Broadmoor, but thought an insanity plea would save him from being hanged. Margaret, desperately in love with him and quite amoral, came in on his side—Arthur knew nothing about that. If Latimer were caught, Margaret's job was just to kill the remaining relations, and so 'prove' that Latimer wasn't the killer, because the killer was still abroad. It wasn't so good in practice as in theory, and she spoiled it by making the fatal mistake of being caught.

"She must have been crazy when she went to Birmingham," went on Roger, "although whether it'll come within the legal meaning of insanity I don't know. I hope not. She knew where the gun was—in a room they rented near Pullinger Street. We found the stolen goods there. Latimer tucked them away to confuse us as much as he could; he was always planting evidence for his defense. They were too smart all along—as when Meg told us about Latimer's drug trafficking, to give a plausible reason why he was on the run.

"The works were nearly upset when Raymond became curious. Raymond had been going to see Arthur Bennett, and saw Latimer in the neighborhood. He guessed that Arthur was on the rocks, and was curious. He watched Arthur very closely; that was what he was doing when he was supposed to be in North Wales. Arthur saw him, and they had a fine old row. Later Latimer and Raymond met by appointment, and Latimer had promised Arthur to do a deal with Raymond, who wasn't averse to cashing in. That's why Raymond lied about where he'd been and what time he got home —he was toying with taking a share, and was jittery. You know how it affects men who are taking a chance for the first time.

"But Latimer believed he would have an easier job with Arthur, and killed Raymond."

Roger stopped and stubbed out the cigarette. Chatworth pushed the box across the table.

"Satisfied?" Chatworth asked.

"Perfectly."

"No more snags?"

"I don't think we'll find any." Roger was as confident as he seemed. "It was cunningly conceived, but began to fall to pieces because Latimer wasn't clever enough. He saw the danger after killing Wilfred, and instead of brazening it out, went into hiding and began to confuse the trails. He started making a 'defense'—having in mind that Meg would kill if he were caught; he knew he could rely on her. Latimer did the first two jobs and then went and robbed the homes of his victims, to make it look as if robbery were the motive. It started well, and put us off the scent. He didn't reckon on Muriel Arlen naming him so early—his big mistake was letting the affair with Muriel run on. There's probably something in his claim that he is in love with her—he didn't really hurt her when he attacked her at Merrick Street."

Chatworth grunted.

"No. Seen Margaret Sharp again?"

"I spent ten minutes with her, and she won't say a word, but I don't think we'll need her evidence just yet. We've enough from the statements of Latimer and Arthur Bennett to piece everything together. Arthur started by trying to blame his brother, but that didn't last long. Anything else you'd like explained, sir?"

Chatworth said: "Yes. Why did you start probing into Simon Arlen's fortune and into the financial state of Bennett Brothers?"

"I was looking for a motive which wasn't a simple matter of a man going off his head. Latimer's behavior wasn't consistent—I wondered if he were putting on an act. Margaret Sharp wasn't normal, and she showed clear signs of disliking her sister because her sister was doing better. Meg had gone through her own money. Envy, and touched by greed—money's usually a pretty sound motive. The red herrings of their dual personalities and the mystery man who never existed pointed away from insanity. They invented the mystery man at Pullinger Street, of course—as we got closer, they started wild attempts to fool us—going from one to another. Meg always defended Latimer to Georgina, of course—even told her he was going to pay back some of his debt.

"When it proved that there was a reasonable chance that Simon had never really been insane, but just put away so that the others could cash in, things began to make sense. The terms of the wills suggested that one of Simon's generation was involved. After that, it was a simple matter of sifting through them all until one turned up who fitted."

"I see," grunted Chatworth. "And I suppose you're feeling pretty pleased with yourself."

The trial was over, and Latimer and Margaret had both been sentenced to death, Arthur to fifteen years' imprisonment.

Roger drove home from the Yard on the evening of the last day of the trial, but didn't go straight to Bell Street. There was no one outside the Arlen house in Merrick Street. He hadn't seen Mrs. Wilfred Arlen in court, and wondered if she had gone out of town.

The manservant answered his ring.

Mrs. Arlen was at home....

She looked younger and much less careworn

than when he had seen her before; and happier. She looked surprised to see him, but didn't ask him why he'd come. She offered cigarettes, let him light hers, and sat down and waited.

"How is Dennis?" asked Roger.

"He's surprisingly well," said Mrs. Arlen. "I was afraid it would make him worse, but there's a good chance that he'll grow out of his heart trouble if he's well looked after in the next few years. Don't tell me that's why you came."

"Chiefly. How are you?"

She said: "You're a strange man for a policeman, aren't you? Do you care how I am?"

"I'd hate to see anyone pining because of Ralph Latimer."

"I'm over that," she said quietly. "You'll probably think it's a hateful thing to say, but—I'm completely free now. Wilfred's just a memory, not pleasant, not really unpleasant. It's more like a dream than a memory."

As Roger drove off, he was smiling, glad that he'd taken the trouble to call.

He was home in time to give the boys half an hour's ride before bedtime.

Two months later Georgina Sharp opened the door of the flat, said: "Hallo, Jim," and stepped aside. Peel passed her. He had seen little of her since the final arrests and the executions. She had been a witness, of course, and had stood that ordeal well. She looked tired and pale, but her easy grace of movement hadn't deserted her. She offered him cigarettes and took a light from him, so that they stood very close together.

"I hoped you'd come," she said.

"I waited as long as I could. I don't have to watch myself with you now."

"Did you ever?"

"Yes, up to a point," said Peel. "I didn't ask you to marry me, did I?" He was smiling slightly, but couldn't hide his tension.

She smiled, too. "Ought you to, now? I'm the sister of a woman who was hanged."

"What's that got to do with it?"

"You *are* a policeman."

"Meaning that I'll spend part of my life chasing murderers and getting them hanged?"

"Meaning that all the time you'd be remembering that my sister was—"

"Listen," said Peel vigorously; "you're talking out of the back of your neck."

He tossed his cigarette into the fireplace, and slid his arm round her, drew her close and found her lips.

By the year 2000, 2 out of 3 Americans could be illiterate.

It's true.

Today, 75 million adults...about one American in three, can't read adequately. And by the year 2000, U.S. News & World Report envisions an America with a literacy rate of only 30%.

Before that America comes to be, you can stop it...by joining the fight against illiteracy today.

Call the Coalition for Literacy at toll-free **1-800-228-8813** and volunteer.

**Volunteer
Against Illiteracy.
The only degree you need
is a degree of caring.**

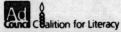 Ad Council Coalition for Literacy

THIS AD PRODUCED BY MARTIN LITHOGRAPHERS
A MARTIN COMMUNICATIONS COMPANY